THE HEART'S HOSTAGE

"I'd like to know why you decided to abduct me," Amanda demanded abruptly. "You don't seem to be very experienced at this business."

The highwayman's pale eyes glinted. "Indeed? Pray, tell me what I ought to do now, according to your lurid imagination? Bind and blindfold you? . . . I should really be concerned about that unruly temper of yours."

Amanda drew an angry breath. "Well, I'd far rather have a temper than be a cold fish like you, with no human emotions!"

"Is that so?" Nick's eyes glittered with sudden anger. Then, without warning, he jerked her hard against his chest, and covered her mouth in a fierce kiss. The world spun dizzyingly until she was abruptly released. "There, was that cold enough for you?"

Amanda stared blindly. By all rights, she ought to have felt frightened, but instead she felt an enervating warmth spreading through her body. Even though Nick's kiss was no more than a gesture of anger, it had somehow turned everything upside down . . .

THE TIMELESS CHARM OF ZEBRA'S REGENCY ROMANCES

CHANGE OF HEART (3278, $3.95)
by Julie Caille

For six years, Diana Farington had buried herself in the country, far from the gossip surrounding her ill-fated marriage and her late husband's demise. When she reluctantly returns to London to oversee her sister's debut, she vows to hold her head high. The behavior of the dangerously handsome Lord Lucan, was too much to bear. Diana knew that she could only expect an improper proposal from the rake, and she was determined that *no* man, let alone Lord Lucan, would turn her head again.

The Earl of Lucan knew that second chances were rare, so when he saw the golden-haired Diana again after so many years, he swore he would win her heart this time around. She had lost her innocence over the years, but he swore he could make her trust — and love — again.

THE HEART'S INTRIGUE (3130, $2.95)
by Evelyn Bond

Lady Clarissa Tregallen preferred the solitude of Cornwall to the ballrooms and noisy routs of the London *ton,* but the future bride of the tediously respectable Duke of Mainwaring would soon be forced to enter Society. To this she was resigned — until her evening walk revealed a handsome, wounded stranger. Bryan Deverell was certainly a spy, but how could she turn over a wounded man to the local authorities?

Deverell planned to take advantage of the beauty's hospitality and be on his way once he recovered, yet he found himself reluctant to leave his charming hostess. He would prove to this very proper lady that she was also a very *passionate* one, and that a scoundrel such as he could win her heart.

SWEET PRETENDER (3248, $3.95)
by Violet Hamilton

As the belle of Philadelphia, spirited Sarah Ravensham had no fondness for the hateful British. But as a patriotic American, it was her duty to convey a certain document safely into the hands of Britain's prime minister — even if it meant spending weeks aboard ship in the company of the infuriating Britisher of them all, the handsome Col. Lucien Valentine.

Sarah was unduly alarmed when her cabin had been searched. But when she found herself in the embrace of the arrogant Colonel — and responding to his touch — she realized the full extent of the dangers she was facing. Not the least of which was the danger to her own impetuous heart . . .

Amanda's Folly

Elizabeth Morgan

ZEBRA BOOKS
KENSINGTON PUBLISHING CORP.

ZEBRA BOOKS

are published by

Kensington Publishing Corp.
475 Park Avenue South
New York, NY 10016

First printing: December, 1991

Printed in the United States of America

Chapter One

The sharp explosion of sound cracked the still-ness of the autumn evening. In the next instant, the carriage came to a jerking halt, its occupants colliding violently against one another before falling back against the stiffly padded cushions.

"Is anyone injured?" A young woman's voice, urgent with concern, rose above the din of stifled shrieks. "Chloe, my love, have you been hurt?"

"N-no, I'm all right," a much younger girl answered shakily. "My wrist smarts a bit, nothing more."

"What of you, Jenny?"

"Only a bruise or two, Miss Amanda, but what in the Lord's name—"

"Hush then!" The command was soft-spoken but firm. "I must listen!"

In the obedient silence which followed, they could hear the noise of the horses snorting and stamping in the chill night air, and the gruffness of men's voices. Then there came a sudden shout of laughter and the clear, ringing words:

"By Jove, I almost forgot! I'm supposed to say 'stand and deliver'!"

The three women froze, staring at each other in dismay. Highwaymen! They all knew what that could mean. There could scarcely be a soul the length and breadth of England who had not heard rumors of the Fitzhugh Gang, who were terrorizing the Brighton Road, or of Gentleman Bob, who had murdered a man near Hampstead in broad daylight. There were other tales, even more lurid, which had found their way to the servants' hall; with a noiseless sigh, the terrified abigail sank back in a dead faint.

Miss Chloe Waverley reached out instinctively to clutch at her stepsister's hands, and as Miss Amanda Waverley felt the younger girl tremble, she forced herself to speak with a calmness that she was far from feeling. "Don't worry, pet," she said reassuringly, "they won't harm us. When they see how little we have, they'll soon depart."

Even as she spoke the words, the elder Miss Waverley knew how false that hope could be. In contrast to her sister, who had not yet left the schoolroom, she was experienced enough to know that once their identity was revealed, robbery would be the least of their worries. Fear for herself, however, was overshadowed by her protective concern for the younger girl, whose fragile beauty far outshone Miss Waverley's own modest charms. At that moment, she wished fervently that she had some sort of weapon at hand, but although many gentlemen's coaches were equipped with pistols on the inside, the Waverleys' ancient vehicle possessed none. Under present circumstances, she could only try to use her own wits, assuage Chloe's fear, and hope for the best.

With an effort, she summoned all the assurance of her twenty-three years, and gave Chloe's hands an encouraging squeeze. "We shall remember this as a great adventure!" she whispered. Then she settled back stiffly against the cushions to wait for what must come; only the rapid pulse beating at the base of her throat revealed the terrible tension which gripped her.

The door of the carriage was suddenly thrown open. "You there!" a coarse voice growled. "Get out where we can see you!" With only the merest hesitation, Miss Waverley gathered her skirts and descended carefully, steadfastly ignoring the man's whistle of surprise. She then reached back to assist Chloe, taking good care that the girl's cloak and hood concealed her well. It was only then that she took a deep breath and turned around to face the enemy.

She found herself staring up at a horseman, a tall, lean silhouette against the night sky. He was mounted on a stallion whose sloping neck and tapered legs gave evidence of Arabian blood; such a horse was so strikingly out of place that it was a moment before she raised surprised eyes to scan the figure of the man himself. When she did so, she saw that he was long-limbed, probably quite tall, and attired in black, from the low-brimmed hat pulled down over a half-mask, to the soles of his gleaming black boots. One elegantly pale hand held the reins with indifferent assurance, and in the other there glinted a silver-mounted pistol, which was pointed straight at her heart.

"There be another wench in there, guv'nor, but she be out cold." The coarse voice boomed directly behind her, with startling force. There must be two of the ruffians at least, she realized, a situation which dimmed her hopes of escape. She could not allow her dismay to be seen, however, and her chin went up slightly in unconscious challenge.

The horseman smiled, and his white teeth gleamed briefly in the darkness. "Leave the other one alone for the moment, Teddy. You'd best keep an eye on the coachman, while I examine the rest of the merchandise."

He then turned to give a small nod in the direction of the two girls. "Good evening, ladies," he said mockingly. "Pray accept my apologies for incommoding you."

The horseman's voice was deep and unexpectedly cultured, but Miss Waverley scarcely noticed. She was aware only that he was toying with them, obtaining some perverted amusement from their helplessness, and her independent nature asserted itself in rising indignation.

"Think nothing of it," she replied steadily, with only the merest trace of sarcasm. "It's so delightful to make new acquaintances."

The horseman's mouth compressed suddenly, and he allowed his gaze to wander over Miss Waverley's defiant figure as if truly seeing her for the first time. At the end of his scrutiny, however, he seemed to shrug, as if what he saw left him totally unmoved. And indeed, in her plain, well-worn clothing, she was an unprepossessing sight.

He spoke again, in slightly fatigued tones. "Much as I regret it, ladies, I am here on business. Shall we begin with your jewelry?"

Miss Waverley made no attempt to resist, since any such effort would clearly be futile, as long as that silver pistol was still pointed squarely in her direction. With only a slight trembling in her fingers—which might have been from anger as much as from fear—she managed to unfasten the small gold locket and chain hanging around her neck, the only piece of jewelry she possessed. She then proffered her palm in his direction.

He made no move to reach for it, however, and a contemptuous smile twisted his mouth. "You may keep your pitiful little trinket," he said dismissively. "I have not yet sunk to robbing poor relations or abigails, whichever you may be."

A flush stained Miss Waverley's cheeks, but she managed to quell the sharp words which rose to her lips. There was nothing to be gained by puffing off her family's importance, and perhaps there might be a good deal to lose. She therefore remained silent, refastening the simple chain around her neck.

The horseman addressed his companion impatiently. "What about the other one? Let's see her, Teddy." Before Miss Waverley could move to intervene, the man standing behind them had reached out, tugging back the hood which had concealed Chloe's face. Then his mouth fell open in an audible gasp of surprise.

The moonlight illuminated every detail of Chloe's heart-shaped face, framed by fashionably dusky curls. Her soft blue eyes were wide with terror, and tears sparkled on the tips of her long lashes. Even her figure was perfection itself, as the cloak fell away to reveal her slender curves, molded by the finely woven muslin gown.

In one swift step, Miss Waverley moved to stand beside her, blocking the girl from view. Quickly she unfastened Chloe's necklace of pearls, but when she turned to hand them to the horseman, she saw that he had already dismounted. He seemed to have forgotten her presence as he moved towards Chloe with long graceful strides. He halted before her, grasping her chin and tilting it upwards. "Oho! A diamond of the first water!" he murmured softly, with a little smile in his voice which disturbed Miss Waverley far more than the pistol he still carried.

"What you want is not diamonds, but pearls," she announced coolly, holding up the strand to divert his attention. The highwayman did not release Chloe, but he turned his head, and for a moment his glance was locked upon her stepsister. His eyes gleamed strangely pale in the dim light, and for a moment she felt pierced by his cold assessing stare. He lazily reached to lift the pearls from her fingers, but then his eyes returned to Chloe's face, and Miss Waverley knew with dismay that her challenge had failed.

A deafening report suddenly split the air, and Miss Waverley whirled around to see the other ruffian staggering to the ground. Wilson, the coachman, was standing on the box of the carriage, with smoke curling from the mouth of his weapon. Distracted by Chloe's beauty, the thief had let down his guard, and the coachman had taken good advantage. Before he could take aim once more, however, the tall highwayman had stepped back from Chloe, jerked his silver pistol upwards, and fired. The coachman fell back with a groan.

"Wilson!" Gathering her skirts in haste, and without thought to her own danger, Miss Waverley rushed forward and clambered up the box, barely in time to keep the coachman's swaying body from pitching forward to the ground. She had known him since she was a little girl, and he had always remained loyal and respectful toward her, despite the despised position she held in her stepmother's household. And now he had risked his life to save her! Anger at this fresh outrage surged briefly within her, and as she propped the coachman gently against the seat, she directed a fulminating glance towards the highwayman below.

"'Tis just my arm, Miss Waverley." Wilson's voice came in breathless gasps. "But I'm sorry I couldn't—I didn't—"

"Save your strength," she urged softly. It was indeed only a graze, as she saw with relief, and it was the work of a moment to bind it up securely with the man's kerchief. "I shan't forget your bravery. Now, please lie down and keep your arm quite still for a few moments." He was only too glad to do as he was bid, and Miss Waverley turned to find herself closely observed by the man whose presence she had almost forgotten. She began to clamber down from the high box of the carriage, but before she reached the ground, she heard a soft approach behind her and felt a firm pair of hands clasp her waist, lifting her bodily into the air before setting her on her feet. Flushing at this brief but ignominious contact, Miss Waverley looked up into the face of her accoster.

Standing so close, she was painfully conscious of his unusual height, as her head barely grazed the level of his chin, though her own stature was by no means diminutive. It gave her a most unwelcome sense of disadvantage. "That was most unnecessary, sir," she snapped, although the statement earned her only an ironic bow.

"As you wish, madam," he smiled insolently. "But did I hear that servant mention the name of Waverley?"

"My name is no concern of yours!" was her retort, in the most discouraging tone she could muster.

He contemplated her for a moment, as if gauging the strength of her resistance, and then shrugged. "You may not wish to tell me, madam. But I think this lady will." Miss Waverley's attention was suddenly recalled to her stepsister's trembling figure, as the highwayman stepped closer to the girl and tilted her chin towards him. "What is your name, my lovely?" he coaxed with soft menace, homing in on her obvious fear.

Chloe was oblivious of Miss Waverley's frantic

gesture behind the man's back. Like a small animal mesmerized by a snake, she stared into his face and whispered faintly. "Chloe Elaine Waverley."

"So." The highwayman stepped back, releasing her. "Daughter of Sir Ian Waverley?"

"Y-yes," she faltered.

"A good family, you should be proud." The highwayman sounded quite pleased with himself, and the elder Miss Waverley tensed, suddenly wary. "And no doubt they will pay handsomely for your return."

Chloe stared at him uncomprehendingly, but her stepsister's wits were far more quick. "You can't do that!" she exclaimed in outrage.

"Can't I just?" he challenged, and before her horrified eyes he reached down and swept Chloe up into his arms. In a few swift strides he carried her to his horse, tossing her lightly into the saddle and swinging himself up behind her. The girl had now realized what was happening, and she was whimpering, almost hysterical with terror.

"No! I beg you!" Miss Waverley cried out, instantly forgetting her pride in a wave of near-panic. "Don't take her, she's so young—only sixteen!"

For a moment the horseman frowned, as he felt the shuddering sobs racking Chloe's delicate frame. "So young as that?" he asked ruefully. "Well, it can't be helped. I must have Miss Waverley, or there's no ransom."

"Then take me instead!" The words rang out

with impassioned clarity. "I am Miss Waverley also—in fact, the elder Miss Waverley. My ransom would be worth far more!"

The horseman was suddenly very still in the saddle. "You do a brave thing, madam," he said quietly. "But why should I believe you? Elder sisters don't dress in rags, while younger ones parade themselves in finery."

"Why not?" she retorted. "I have been on the shelf these five years past, while Chloe is on the verge of her comeout. Besides," she added, unable to prevent a hint of desperation from coloring her voice, "they cannot possibly raise the money before tomorrow. This episode would wreck her chances for a good match, even if you returned her safe in the morning. I have no such chances to wreck. Please, if you must take one of us, I beg you to let her go and take me."

There was a moment of pregnant silence, and then wordlessly the horseman dismounted, gently lowering Chloe to the ground. She collapsed sobbing into her stepsister's arms, allowing herself to be helped into the safety of the carriage, where Jenny still lay in a faint. The highwayman was meanwhile scribbling a short letter, obviously a ransom note, and when he had done, his glance fastened upon the small reticule dangling from Miss Waverley's wrist. "Give me that," he ordered curtly. "It will serve as proof that you were taken unwillingly."

She handed it to him without protest; this last indignity scarcely seemed to matter, when she was facing only heaven knew what in this man's

14

hands. For one paralyzing moment she regretted her rash offer, and her mouth almost opened to plead for mercy. But then she recalled the hardness in his eyes, and the firm set of his jaw. There would be no mercy from him, and as long as he was determined to hold one of them for ransom, she would not give him the satisfaction of seeing her trepidation.

He thrust the note inside the bag, and then tossed it into Chloe's lap as she huddled against the cushions. "Make sure that you deliver this when you get home, my lovely. If your coachman can't drive, this is a well-travelled road; someone should be by quite soon to find you."

"What about your—your friend?" Miss Waverley could not help asking him, with an uneasy glance over her shoulder.

He threw back his head and laughed, a chilling sound. "Let him rot. He didn't do the job I engaged him for."

Miss Waverley's eyes flickered slightly at his callousness, and he looked down at her with a disturbing smile. "Changing your mind so soon, Miss Waverley?" he taunted. "It's not too late to use my original plan. And besides, your sister is by far the more delectable armful."

She tilted her head back to meet his eyes, stung by the jibe. "You are despicable, sir," she hissed softly.

His only answer was to seize her by the waist once more, this time very ungently, and to toss her up onto the saddle of his horse. A moment later he was up behind her, his arms snaked under hers to hold the reins. She stiffened involuntarily at the contact, but his left arm curled around her waist and forced her back against him.

"This will be damned uncomfortable enough without you making it worse," he growled. Then he touched his heels to the flanks of his horse, and they bolted forward into the darkness.

Chapter Two

The pounding of the horse's hooves and the shifting of its powerful withers created a pulsating rhythm, and as the miles slowly rolled by, Miss Waverley found her fears gradually lulled into a strange feeling of calm. In contrast to the coldness of the night air, she felt instinctively warmed and somehow protected by the supporting arms of the man behind her. Only once before in her life had she known the comfort of such an embrace, and that brief and innocent delight had brought disaster in its wake.

Wearied by the fatigue and tension she had struggled to conceal, and still imprisoned in the highwayman's secure hold, she soon forgot her determination to watch for landmarks. Instead, her eyelids slowly began to droop. Peter would hold her safe, she knew, and his shoulder was so broad beneath her cheek . . .

She awoke with a start to find that the horse had stopped moving, and she was being grasped under the arms by a pair of strong hands. For a moment she was completely disoriented, until she found herself being pulled from the saddle and lowered unceremoniously to the ground. Then all at once she recalled her abduction. She ought to be terrified; perversely, however, she was aware of a sense of abandonment now that those comforting arms were no longer holding her.

"What's wrong? Why have we stopped?" she protested, rocking sleepily on her feet as the highwayman dismounted with easy grace.

"We've arrived," was the curt reply.

"Arrived where?" she persisted.

He stopped in the act of loosening the saddle girths to glance at her quizzically over his shoulder. "All you need to know, my dear, is that this is where we spend the night."

They were standing before a large cottage, its sloping thatched roof half-hidden by overhanging tree limbs that swayed menacingly in the wind. Moonlight reflected off the panes of its small windows, partly obscured by climbing ivy. The entire aspect was deserted and forbidding, and Amanda could not repress a shudder. Beyond all doubt, this was the perfect setting for a violent crime.

"Well, what are you waiting for?" the highwayman said irritably, interrupting the morbid train of her thoughts. "Go inside, and I'll join you after I give Darius a rubdown."

Miss Waverley did not wait to be told twice. She pushed open the door with some trepidation, hardly daring to imagine the squalors of this thieves' den, but the moonlight revealed only a single spacious room, furnished with a large oak table and chairs, a plain wooden sideboard, and a small wardrobe. The air was thick with a musty smell, and when she ran a finger over the tabletop, she could feel the grit of dust. Clearly this place was not often used as a rendezvous.

She turned to peer through the darkness at the far end of the room, and was rewarded with the sight of a narrow bed wedged against the wall. There was no other bed in sight, however, and that fact was sufficient to banish any trace of lingering sleepiness which she might have been feeling. Try as she might to stay calm, Miss Waverley could not master the cold knot of tension forming in her stomach.

As her eyes became accustomed to the darkness, she saw a tinderbox and candles upon the mantelpiece. After one or two fumbling attempts, when her nervous fingers simply refused to cooperate, she managed to strike a flame, anxious to calm herself with light, if not heat. She lit the candles and then forced herself to sit down on a chair, lacing her fingers together in her lap to stop their trembling. I have nothing to fear, she reassured herself, even if I am alone with him, miles from anywhere, and no one could hear me if . . . Determinedly she wrenched her thoughts away from that very unproductive direction. Instead, she tried to concentrate on memorizing her surroundings, so that eventually she would be able to bring the culprit to justice.

The front latch rattled, the door swung open

with a faint creak, and the subject of her thoughts walked in. She noted that he had to stoop slightly to enter; then he straightened his tall frame and raised his arms in a long stretch, easing his tired limbs.

"Bloody cold in here, isn't it?" he announced brusquely, and her mouth tightened at his language. "I'll light the fire." She watched as he knelt before the hearth, and within a few minutes the room began to come alive with the sound and warmth of crackling flames. Miss Waverley pulled her chair closer to the fire, but could not yet control her shivering.

"Here's what you need." She turned her head to see the highwayman remove a bottle and glasses from the sideboard. With a quick gust of breath, he blew away the dust which had settled in the glasses, and then he poured out two generous measures of a noxious-looking liquid. He thrust one glass in her direction.

Miss Waverley recoiled. "No, I—"

"Drink it." It was not a request, but an order, and she quelled the urge to defy him. She accepted the glass reluctantly, but after the first hesitant sip, she realized that it was only brandy. She had to admit that its stinging warmth was welcome, although it was a struggle not to cough. Either the taste of vintage brandy was one which she had too long been denied, or else the bottle had half turned to vinegar.

The highwayman pulled up another chair and leaned back, his booted legs stretched out before him. In the flickering light of the fire, Miss

Waverley could see his face for the first time without the hat and mask.

He was younger than she had supposed, perhaps about twenty-eight or twenty-nine, and his features were handsome, but rather sharply chiseled, with a long thin nose and a cynical twist to his mouth. Silvery blond hair fell in disordered short locks, and his eyes were oddly pale, either gray or green; she could not quite tell in the dim light. His build was lean, but the width of his shoulders owed nothing to the tailor's art, and she knew well enough from their previous contact that his muscles were hard and athletic.

As he flexed his hands towards the fire, seemingly oblivious of her scrutiny, she noted with some surprise the exquisite cut of his riding coat of black merino, the tight fit of his breeches, and the polished sheen of his glove-soft leather boots. Even considering her limited acquaintance of highwaymen, this ruffian seemed to be dressed with extraordinary attention to fashion.

Tossing off the last of his brandy, he folded his arms negligently behind his head and suddenly turned his head, fixing Miss Waverley with an insolent stare. She met his gaze for a brief startled moment, and then dropped her eyes before the cold intensity of his regard. Pointedly she turned away to face the hearth, determined to appear indifferent to his stare.

In the warm glow of the firelight, the highwayman slowly scanned Miss Waverley's figure from head to foot, and her appearance took him somewhat by surprise. Previously he had thought her quite unremarkable, but though her clothes were unmistakably dowdy, she was by no means plain. The firelight was kind to her disarrayed honey brown hair, lending it a bronzed sheen which matched the glowing color of her eyes. Nor could any serious fault be found with her finely molded features, though perhaps her straight nose was a shade too long, and her well-shaped mouth a bit too large to fit the fashionable ideal. But it was an expressive face, with an arresting quality that somehow drew and held one's notice. And despite that abominable cloak and gown, he could see that her neck was long and slender, and her carriage graceful. This female was definitely not in his style, but his interest was piqued nonetheless.

"What is your name?" he asked suddenly, making her jump. Her startled expression narrowed to one of suspicion when she saw the disquieting gleam in his eyes.

"You know it, sir," she replied frostily.

"No," he insisted, "I mean your first name."

Miss Waverley raised her chin defiantly. "I find your question unnecessary and impertinent," she stated with hauteur.

His smile was ominous. "On the scale of possible impertinence, my dear, that question hardly rates. Shall I demonstrate something more worthy of the term?"

"No, thank you!" she hastened to reply. "Very well, if you must know, my given name is Amanda."

"Amanda." He repeated the word softly, almost to himself. "'To be loved.'" His eyes raked her once more, and then he shrugged slightly and looked away, returning his attention to the brandy bottle and pouring himself another healthy measure. "Well, I suppose appearances can be deceiving."

Miss Waverley stiffened from his casual insult. "True enough, sir," she said silkily, "after all, you have every appearance of being a gentleman."

His mouth twitched slightly, but whether with anger or amusement she could not tell. "With that tongue of yours, I don't wonder that you've received no offers." His tone was odiously patronizing, and her temper flared.

"I have had several offers!" she retorted, immediately regretting her outburst when his eyebrows lifted in surprise.

"Why aren't you married, then?" he countered.

She hesitated only a moment before answering, in what she hoped was a quelling tone, "I simply had no wish to accept any of the offers I received."

He shook his head in disbelief. "I never met a female who wasn't mad to tie the knot. Were you hanging out for a title, or did you cherish some romantic notion of finding true love?"

His words were sarcastic, and Miss Waverley kept her face expressionless, but her stiff posture and the tightly clenched fingers in her lap betrayed a reaction which was all too real.

"So you have been in love after all," he pursued cruelly, watching her movements. "Then it must have been someone who didn't return your affections."

"No!" The word broke from her lips before she

realized, but he could not tell whether it was an agreement or a denial. She faced him once more, her eyes liquid with suppressed emotion. "I'd really rather not discuss my private affairs, if you please."

He met her gaze squarely, but after only a moment he turned aside in evident boredom. "Have it your own way, then. Let's have some more brandy."

As he refilled their glasses, Miss Waverley determined to distract her captor with some questions of her own, before her life history was further dragged out for his casual amusement.

"I'd like to know why you decided to abduct me," she demanded abruptly.

His pale eyes glinted as he glanced up from pouring the liquor. "Why, because you asked me to," he drawled.

"Don't be ridiculous," she said repressively, making him quirk an amused eyebrow. "You don't seem to be very experienced at this business."

"Indeed? How can you tell?" he inquired curiously.

"Well, for one thing, you didn't trouble to blindfold me on the way here, and you haven't tied me up, or made any effort to prevent me from finding out who you—" She broke off suddenly, aghast at her own stupidity. Like an idiot she had just revealed exactly what she was thinking. What would he do now?

The highwayman stared at her for a moment, pressing together the tips of his shapely fingers. Then his lips curled into a mocking smile. "Well, it's equally obvious that you're not a very experienced victim! Pray, tell me what I ought to do now, according to your lurid imagination? Would you feel better if I did bind and blindfold you?"

"I'd rather you didn't, if you don't mind," she uttered somewhat faintly.

Abruptly he rose out of his chair and stood before the hearth, facing away from her. "Damn it all, why must this be so complicated?" he cursed softly. He swung around to face her, leaning one hand upon the low mantelpiece.

"I suppose I may as well tell you the whole, Amanda, since you're quick enough to discover it for yourself, and I don't really fancy tying you up. You're quite right about my lack of experience, because tonight is my first and, no doubt, my only venture as a highwayman." He smiled ruefully, looking suddenly younger. "It was quite diverting, I must say."

"Diverting?" she echoed, forgetting momentarily that he had presumed to use her first name. "You call it diverting when your partner was killed, and you almost murdered my coachman? Not to mention frightening us all half to death?"

"Oh, perhaps I frightened the others," he said dismissively, "but you've been mighty cool, my dear. Don't look for my sympathy. I'm sorry about your coachman, but the other fellow would have gone to the gallows sooner or later."

She could not repress a small shudder, realizing that behind her captor's negligent air lay a ruthless streak which was more dangerous than anything she had yet faced.

"In any case," he continued, "this morning I found myself in rather a uncomfortable position. Not only did I have to fly the country by tomorrow, but I had to raise the ready for my travelling expenses."

"Why?" she could not help inquiring.

His face looked suddenly weary. "Because last night, or rather quite early this morning, I had the misfortune to kill a man." At her shocked expression, he raised one hand in a careless gesture. "Oh, it was all fair and square. Defending my honor, you might say. It was in London, in a private little place off the Strand where the play runs rather deep."

"Do you mean a gambling hell?" she guessed uncertainly.

"Yes, of course," he confirmed, casting her an impatient look. "What else? As I was saying, the play was deep, and I had already pledged a number of vowels, when I perceived that my partner had somehow substituted a different deck. I had to, er, take him to task."

"So you fought a duel and he was killed?"

"Exactly. I could never stand for being cheated, could I? The unfortunate thing is, since this all took place at three o'clock in the morning, and after quite a few bottles of champagne had been consumed, there were several persons who took violent exception to the proceedings. They informed me that the authorities would be notified and charges would be brought against me on Monday morning, tomorrow. That left just enough time to get to the coast, to catch the packet to France by tomorrow afternoon at the latest."

"And what was the difficulty about funds?" Miss Waverley pursued, intrigued in spite of herself.

"Didn't I say? I'd spent the rolls of soft I had with me, and was already punting on tick."

"How much had you lost?"

His pale brows drew together in an effort to recall. "What on earth does that matter? It was about twelve thousand pounds, I suppose."

She gasped audibly. Twelve thousand pounds? Why, that was a fortune! How could he lose that much money and stand there so calmly?

"Don't look so shocked, my dear," he mocked. "I'll not tell you all the details, but I could afford to lose it."

"How?" she protested. "How could you even have that much money to pledge, when you live in a place like this?"

He tilted his fair head and eyed her quizzically. "You are an innocent, aren't you? This isn't my home, it's only a hunting box belonging to a friend."

Miss Waverley suffered this mortifying rebuke and begged his pardon. "But, in any case, why this masquerade? Had you no one to lend you assistance?"

To her surprise, the highwayman's expression became slightly sheepish, and he cleared his throat before answering. "Fact is, for all that my aim with a pistol was true, I really was a bit under the

27

hatches. By the time my head cleared enough to think of that, I'd been riding hell-bent for leather for two hours. I couldn't afford the time or the risk to turn round and go back in broad daylight. Besides, the notion of playing highwayman hit me, and of course I could not resist."

"Of course not," Miss Waverley echoed drily.

"If it's any consolation," he continued nonchalantly, "I did not plan an abduction. It was hardly my fault if there were so few coaches on the road tonight—too cold, I suppose. And I had the devil of a time finding that oaf to assist me. Your coach was the first one which passed; how was I to know it held only a gaggle of hysterical females with no money or jewels, but for a trumpery string of pearls? I had to take one of you, or else stand by the side of the road the rest of the night, hoping for a better prey to come along before someone gave the alarm in the nearest town."

"And your sense of honor made no protest?"

Her companion gave a short laugh, but there was no humor in the sound. "It was my sense of honor that got me into this mess to begin with, and all over a blasted pack of cards. I'll own I should have acted differently, but you're here now, and as long as your ransom is all that stands between me and the threat of a noose, I'd as lief postpone this discussion of honor to a later date." He stifled a yawn and consulted a handsome gold pocket watch. "Here now, it's getting late. Finish your brandy; it's time to go to bed."

She froze in her chair.

"Don't flatter yourself, Amanda," he said mockingly, reading the thought in her expressive eyes. "You're not such an ill-favored piece as I first thought, but your charms don't tempt me to ravishment. I've got to rise early tomorrow to collect your ransom, and I don't fancy missing another night's sleep." As if to emphasize his words, he calmly sat down upon the bed and began tugging at his boots.

Miss Waverley's gaze travelled from the narrow bed to the uncompromising expression upon her captor's face. "What about me?" she forced herself to ask.

He didn't even spare her a glance. "Well, the most practical thing would be to dispense with maidenly modesty and share the bunk with me. Two bodies are much warmer than one, you know."

"I do not! I mean, I will not! If you refuse to give me the bed, I shall sleep in this chair!"

It was clear from his shrug that he had no intention of doing the gentlemanly thing. "You'll please yourself, of course. But there's only one blanket, and you'll share it with me or do without. I'm afraid I'm not cast in the heroic mould."

Her eyes flashed angrily at this callousness, but if that was how he chose to behave, she was left with no alternative but to draw her cloak more tightly around herself and huddle back into the chair. She could only hope to be spared a dangerous chill.

Conquering his other boot at last, the highwayman looked up to see her glaring at him, and his pale eyes narrowed in amusement. "Don't you want to take off that dress?" he asked with sudden mischieviousness. "You'll get it sadly crumpled."

She bristled visibly, just as he had anticipated. "Your concern is touching," was the icy reply, "but I'll keep it on just the same. No doubt the extra warmth will be welcome."

"Well, then, pleasant dreams, my sweet." And with that cheerful valediction, he stretched out full length upon his back, tucked the single thin blanket around himself, and closed his eyes—but not before Miss Waverley had seen him slip the silver-mounted pistol securely beneath the pillow.

The morning sunlight gradually forced its way into Amanda's consciousness, and her eyes fluttered open. She stretched, yawning, and stared blankly at the ceiling as she tried to recapture fragments of her dream. There had been a wild midnight ride, and a dead man upon the road, and something about a glistening string of pearls . . .

"So you're awake at last," a familiar voice drawled nearby, and she sat up, startled nearly out of her skin. It was no dream, but reality, and unwelcome memories came flooding back. The only question was how she came to be now upon the bed; during the night, her abductor must have taken pity upon her plight, and exchanged places, laying her sleeping form upon the bed and covering her with the blanket. Then he must have taken her place in the chair—or so she fervently hoped!

"I trust you slept well," he continued, discarding his greatcoat and settling himself into a chair opposite her. It was evident that he had been outside, though for how long, she had no notion. "Because if you're quite awake, there's something we must discuss." The tone of his voice made her feel suddenly chill.

"I've already been to the place where I instructed your family to leave the ransom. I deliberately asked for rather a small sum, so that they would be certain to have it in the house. But there was no money. There was this letter instead, the contents of which may interest you."

Though he was not looking at her, his voice was openly sardonic now, and she could only murmur her willingness to listen, wondering at the cause of his strange mood as he began to read aloud.

"To Whom It May Concern: Being in receipt of your outrageous demand, and witnessing the suffering which you have brutally inflicted upon an innocent young girl, I hearby inform you that never shall you receive one penny of the funds which have been entrusted to me. As for my stepdaughter, I am convinced that this incident was provoked by her own immodest and shocking behavior, which she has amply demonstrated in the past, and which has brought dishonor to her name. Henceforth she is no longer a member of this family, and is forbidden to set foot upon this property. I desire never to see her or hear her name again. Signed, Ruth, Lady Waverley."

Amanda sat perfectly still, and a wave of faintness washed over her, leaving her face very pale. The silence stretched as the cruel words slowly sank into her brain. She had always known that her stepmother despised her, but even so, the spiteful words came as a shock. And what would become of her now, with no home, however hateful it might have been, to which she could return?

Her abductor's voice interrupted these painful thoughts, forcing her to look up and face him. "I think you'd better give me an explanation, Amanda. What the devil is going on here?"

Was that pity in his tone, or merely frustration at this fresh obstacle to his plan of escape? It was impossible to know, and there was certainly no need for her to tell this stranger the truth, but there was something in his gaze which seemed to compel honesty, as if he could actually read into her soul. Amanda felt a sudden longing to be done with all pretense, and after taking a deep breath, she began to speak in a low voice.

"You may as well know that I haven't exactly been on the shelf these past years. In fact, I've been in disgrace over a young man." Wrapped in her memories, Amanda was unaware of her captor's start of surprise. "His name was Peter Barnett, and he was the son of the Squire. We practically grew up together, since our lands marched side by side, and I was rather a wild little girl." She smiled ruefully in remembrance. "My mother died when I was quite young, and I used to climb trees and run footraces with all the boys of the neighborhood, no matter how hard my father tried to make me act the young lady. Peter was only a year older than I, and he was always there to help me out of scrapes. Then, when I was sixteen, things changed, and . . . we fell in love.

32

"By this time my father had remarried, a widow with a young daughter. Lady Ruth objected to my unladylike behaviour and was always trying to punish me for one thing or another. My father defended me, but within a year he caught a fever, and he died." Amanda had to pause a moment, swallowing back a rush of emotion. "Things got worse and worse. Peter and I desperately wanted to be married, but my stepmother was set on my having a season in London and making a brilliant match." Her tone became bitter. "The son of the Squire wasn't good enough for a Waverley.

"So, I was packed off to London. In the meantime, Peter's father decided to buy him a commission in the Army, and he was sent to Portugal. I received several offers almost at once, but I refused them all; I was going to wait for Peter until I came of age. My stepmother was furious, of course. Then, after about four months—" Amanda stopped abruptly.

"Then?" she was prompted.

"Then Peter was killed." The inevitable tears stung her eyelids and choked her voice to a mere whisper. "I had to stay and finish out the season, but it was rather a social disaster, and my stepmother has never been able to forgive me. I know that she has longed for the opportunity to be rid of me, but I never imagined that she would go as far as this."

There was a pregnant silence. "That's not the whole tale, now, is it," her listener said quietly.

Amanda drew her breath in a little sob, and then shook her head. "No. You see, that last night before Peter and I parted, we were both so miserable and frightened of the future. I slipped out after midnight to meet him in the summerhouse, and we just talked and talked—neither one of us could bear to be the first to say farewell. I finally returned to the house just before daybreak.

"No one was the wiser, until my stepmother searched my wardrobe one day and found one of his letters, in which he spoke of our precious night together.

"We had done nothing but embrace, but my stepmother was of a mind to think the worst. She was so furious that she locked me in my room for a week, and then of course the servants whispered. Very soon after, rumors began to circulate about my mysterious transgression, and invitations came in less frequently. Lady Ruth blamed me for that, and for the fact that I received no new offers, and at the end of the season, I went home in disgrace. And that is where I have remained . . . until now."

There was silence for a long moment. "A very affecting tale," her listener drawled at last, though he handed her his handkerchief. "But for the moment, I'm afraid I must be rather more concerned with how I'm to get the money I need."

"Oh, yes, your money," Amanda echoed contemptuously. "Let us certainly not forget that." She then blew her nose into his handkerchief with a defiant honk. That prosaic action brought the unexpected glimmer of a smile to the lips of a man whose previous experience of weeping women was confined to vaporish female relatives and cajoling mistresses, whose tears glistened entrancingly upon darkened lashes. None of them would ever be so undignified as to mangle a man's handkerchief in such a way.

But these thoughts were quickly dismissed, as he turned his attention back to matters at hand. Crossing to the door, he picked up his greatcoat and pulled it on.

"It appears as though I'll require another inspiration," he mused aloud, examining a spot upon his sleeve. "If all else fails, I can sell my horse, although every finer feeling recoils at the thought. I'd hate to leave the poor brute at the mercy of strangers."

So saying, he glanced up and saw that Miss Waverley had gone very still. There was a stricken look in her tawny eyes, but almost instantly it was veiled behind her lowered lashes. When she spoke, her voice was quite steady.

"I'm certain you will come about, but you had best be gone quickly. Allow me to wish you *bon voyage.*"

For some odd reason, these words touched him in a way that tears or lamentations could never have done. He paused in the act of drawing on his gloves, his pale brows drawn into a frown.

"What will you do now, Amanda?" he asked sharply.

She lifted her chin and met his gaze, determined to maintain her composure no matter what. "That is not your concern, sir," she said coldly.

"Indeed it isn't," he agreed, "but despite my many faults, I'm not such a bloody cur as to go off and leave you here alone. Tell me where you want to go, and if it's within reason, I'll take you there."

Amanda slowly shook her head as if in refusal, and he took an impatient step forward. "Confound your pride, girl," he hissed. "I haven't the time to waste. Where shall I take you? Surely you've some other relative or friend?"

"You don't understand," she said bleakly. "There's nowhere for me to go. For five years my stepmother has kept me apart from the world, and poisoned others against me. Even Squire Barnett refused to answer my letters, and he'd been like a father to me ever since my—" She coughed, trying to clear the tight ache in her throat. "Besides, even if there might be some who remember me with kindness, my stepmother is a very wealthy and powerful woman. I assure you, not even the Vicar would dare risk her anger by offering me a home."

She suddenly pressed her hands to her temples. "Forgive me, but I'm not thinking very clearly at the moment. I'll manage somehow. But you must well and truly be gone from here; no matter what's happened, I don't fancy the thought of you being hanged for murder."

He stared at her assessingly, and then slowly expelled his breath in an exasperated sigh. "Very well, then," he declared. "Put on your cloak; until you or I can think of something better, you'll have to come with me to Paris."

Amanda gasped. "Paris! That's impossible!"

Her abductor's mouth compressed into a mocking smile. "Are you so concerned for your reputation?"

She looked at him in consternation, her thoughts in a whirl. He was right, of course; she had nothing further to lose, and in fact it would be the height of foolishness to refuse his offer of aid, no matter how grudging it may be, or how much her instincts might rebel against it. She'd be better off with the devil she knew than with braving the world alone and penniless. And, of course, it would only be a temporary arrangement.

"Very well," she said at last. "I have no choice but to accept your protection. But will you give me your word that . . ." Her voice trailed off, and she flushed slightly.

He made a grimace, almost of distaste. "That I won't threaten what's left of your precious virtue? You needn't fear, Amanda; I've no designs in that direction." Then his gaze narrowed slowly. "Or have I misunderstood? Did you intend an invitation?"

A fresh flare of temper restored her fragile composure. "Perhaps I have no claim to your respect," she said, willing her voice to remain steady. "And I certainly can't prevent you from insulting me in any fashion you choose. But allow me to say, sir, that although I must be grateful for your assistance in my current predicament, I find that particular insinuation, and you, quite utterly repulsive."

His face twisted in sudden, unwilling amusement. "Good God, that's a most unflattering set-down! Must you truly mean 'repulsive'—wouldn't 'annoying' do just as well?"

It was Amanda's turn to utter a reluctant laugh, but before she could think of an appropriate riposte, he was already striding towards the door. "Come along, then," he called over his shoulder, once more distant and mocking. "Now that we've established our mutual distaste, there's no time to be lost; the packet leaves at four o'clock, and we've a long ride ahead."

Chapter Three

Long before they arrived at the coast, Amanda was cramped and sore from the uncomfortable ride, but not a single word of complaint passed her lips. She had no desire to arouse her companion's cynical irritation; he was already one of the most monstrously selfish individuals she had ever encountered, and despite his momentary generosity, she had no doubt that he was capable of ruthlessly changing his mind and leaving her to her fate. She also had no inclination to provoke his mocking sense of humor, all too often aimed at herself.

All that she permitted to her curiosity was a query as to how to address him, to which he replied curtly that she might call him Nick, and would she be so good as to refrain from prying further into his affairs. It seemed an odd sort of familiarity to be calling him by a given name, whether it be his own or not, but in light of the peculiar situation in which they found themselves, it would be absurdly missish to protest. And as long as he chose to adopt such a rude suspicious manner, she certainly had no wish to burden him with her unwanted conversation. No further words were exchanged until he suggested they stop briefly at a roadside inn, and she agreed with relief.

Nick dismounted and, spanning her waist with his strong fingers, lifted her easily to the ground. He did not release her immediately, but stood looking down at her from his considerable height, his sharp eyes taking in every detail of her windblown hair and flushed cheeks. For a panicked instant she thought he might kiss her; and then he spoke. "You look a frightful mess. Do try to tidy yourself before we go in."

Amanda's eyes had been sparkling with a mixture of dread and helpless anticipation, but now they turned ice-cold. With a barely audible sniff, she turned her back upon him and began to smooth her hair into place, unable to see the amused twist of his mouth.

Nothing could improve the rumpled drabness of her gown, but at least her manner was composed and ladylike as they walked together into the inn. It was a small hostelry, clearly unaccustomed to visiting gentry; its straw-strewn taproom boasted no more than a handful of tables, where several rough-looking locals nursed tankards of the landlord's home-brewed. Those individuals were staring suspiciously at the newcomers, and the atmosphere was unwelcoming in the extreme. Amanda forced herself to take comfort, however, in the fact that no one here was likely to recognize her, or to take particular note of a lady travelling unchaperoned with a gentleman.

Nick paused in the doorway, surveying the scene with an air of distaste. Their host appeared, burly and short, his sleeves rolled up to reveal stocky forearms capable of dealing with even the most unruly customer. He approached, wiping his hands on a dirty apron.

"Good day to ye, sir, madam," the landlord nodded, swiftly assessing their appearance with a practiced eye. Unless he missed his guess, here was a well-breeched swell, plump in the pockets; but the female was plain and poor, most likely a servant or a doxy.

They unwittingly reinforced this error by requesting a private parlor.

"A private parlor, eh?" the man repeated, giving Amanda a sly grin that made her itch to slap his face. Instead, however, she favored him with a haughty stare which sobered him quickly enough. Perhaps he had misjudged the situation, and anyway, lady or lightskirt, it wouldn't do to offend the gent she was with. "Beggin' yer pardon, sir," he replied obsequiously, "but there be no private parlor here."

Nick grimaced slightly. "Very well, then, see if you can find us a clean table. I daresay you have nothing fit to eat, but whatever you've got, I expect to see it quickly. And bring us a bottle of claret, and some lemonade for the lady." Much impressed by these curt commands, and with favorable hopes of a generous compensation, the landlord bowed, motioned them to his best table, bowed again, and then hurried away.

As Nick threw himself into a chair, stretching out his long legs, Amanda could not prevent herself from smiling up at him from under her dark lashes. "Have you no pity for the poor man?" she queried teasingly.

"Pity? Whatever for? I'm damned hungry and thirsty, and I don't like to be kept waiting."

Amanda shook her head reprovingly. "I'm glad I'm not your valet."

"Or my mistress?" Nick's pale eyes glinted with sudden interest. "You needn't worry; I am thought to treat my mistresses very well indeed."

Color rushed into her cheeks. "Have a care, for goodness' sake! Someone might hear you!"

He merely laughed, and before she could think of how to reply, the landlord arrived bearing a tray laden with their refreshments, and conversation was mercifully interrupted.

For the next few minutes, they devoted their attention entirely to the meal. There was only cheese, bread, and cold kidney pie, none too fresh, but neither of them had eaten since the previous day and the food was welcome, poor as it was.

Once the edge of their hunger had dulled, however, the silence stretched uncomfortably. Amanda made a few tentative efforts at conversation, anxious to present a normal appearance to the curious onlookers, but the situation made this extremely difficult. For one thing, she dared not mention their impending journey, being all too conscious of the fact that Nick was an escaping murderer. Furthermore, even the most innocuous questions about Nick were met with such quelling looks that she hastily dropped both her eyes and the subject. Obviously he did not wish to share anything of his private life with her. This was only logical under the circumstances, but the thought still rankled slightly. After all, he knew her own most painful secrets!

Finally their plates were empty, and Nick tossed back the last glass of wine. Amanda noted with relief that the bottle had scarcely affected him, although the color in his normally pale cheeks was slightly heightened.

"We had best be on our way," he said, pulling out his gold timepiece, upon which Amanda now thought she could discern the engraved letters *NM* and a crest of some sort. She knew a momentary curiosity, which was soon stilled by his next words. "There's a goodly distance yet to go, and . . ." His voice trailed off, as he and Amanda were both struck by the same thought. They stared at each other blankly. They had no money with which to pay their bill!

Nick expelled a slow deep breath, murmuring a few words quite unfit for polite company. He closed his eyes, and for a moment his expression was so forbidding that Amanda stifled the sharp words she had been about to utter. Suddenly his taut frame appeared to relax, and when he opened his eyes again they held a gleam which she could not fathom.

"Landlord!" he called out imperiously. "Bring me another bottle!"

Amanda now shut her own eyes in utter disgust.

43

Instead of planning their escape, he was getting himself foxed!

Nick leaned across the table, drawing her attention with a discreet but rather painful pinch of her wrist. "I know what I'm doing, Amanda," he hissed softly. "Now for God's sake try to look as though you were enjoying yourself!"

"Enjoying myself?" she whispered back, glaring at him resentfully. "Certainly I am. And no doubt it will be even more enjoyable to be hauled off to a magistrate, while you lie here in a drunken stupor."

His pale eyes glimmered with comprehension, but his only response was to motion impatiently to the approaching tapster, seizing the bottle off the tray with a slightly unsteady hand.

The next half hour was an excruciating one for Amanda, as her worst fears were realized. In contrast to his earlier silence, Nick now became loquacious, recounting rambling anecdotes of being sent down from Oxford, punctuated by loud laughs which drew the fascinated attention of the room's other occupants. It became increasingly difficult for Amanda to maintain an outward calm, making curt replies when necessary, but although her eyes sparkled with mounting temper, Nick's answering gaze remained bland and quite unresponsive.

The bottle was almost empty, and the tabletop well sprinkled with wine, due to Nick's increased clumsiness, when a seedy-looking individual stood up from a nearby table and began calling out his farewells. Almost at the same moment, Nick pushed himself out of his chair, and stood reeling slightly.

"Time for us to be leaving, m' dear," he announced in a loud slurred voice. Then, at the very moment he turned to reach for his greatcoat, he collided squarely with the departing customer. The other man sprang back, mumbling an oath and rubbing a bruised chin; then he shoved his way past and hurried out the door, leaving Nick blinking in confusion as the onlookers sniggered. Amanda felt ready to sink from humiliation.

Without ceremony, Nick dragged Amanda to her feet and made a clumsy effort to fasten her cloak, remaining oblivious to the scathing expression in her eyes as he turned to seek out the landlord. "Can't wait to get out of this pit! Where's that fellow with our reckoning?" he announced to no one in particular, wavering even more noticeably than before.

Their host was not one to waste such a golden opportunity, and when he materialized at Nick's elbow, he made a rapid calculation. "That'll be eight shillings," he announced craftily.

"Eight shillings! Egad, that's highway robbery!" Nick exclaimed, and despite her rising panic, Amanda had to suppress a bubble of laughter at the irony of his remark. He was a fine one to be accusing anyone of highway robbery!

"Here now, I'll just—I say!" Nick had reached into his waistcoat pocket, and suddenly his eyes widened in angry astonishment. He clapped his hand to his pockets, one after another, but obviously finding nothing. "By God," he roared furiously. "That blackguard's taken my purse!"

A hush fell, broken almost immediately by murmurs from the other customers, as they nodded to each other wisely. So the pigeon had been plucked, had he? One could hardly blame Tom Jenkins; anyone would have done the same, seeing that silly swell drink himself nearly under the table.

"After him! Stop him!" Nick rushed to the door in stumbling haste, tugging Amanda after him with a painful yank on her arm. Leaving the landlord protesting in their wake, he staggered toward their tethered horse and tossed Amanda bruisingly up into the saddle. Moments later, he swung himself up behind her, and spurred his mount into a gallop, bellowing "Stop thief!" as they rapidly put distance between themselves and that accursed inn.

They rode at top speed for several minutes, and then Nick slowed his horse to a walk. "We won't be followed," he announced to Amanda, his voice surprisingly clear and steady. "They won't wish to see their friend caught."

She twisted sharply around on the pommel of his saddle, indignation and relief warring within her. "Of all the lunatic stunts!" she sputtered. "You nearly caused a riot back there! And besides, I was worried to death; why on earth didn't you tell me what you were about?"

His smile was infuriating. "There was no need for you to know. And rest assured, your oh-so-obvious anxiety was quite useful in creating the right atmosphere for my little scheme."

"How dare you!" Amanda fumed. "You had no right to use me in such a despicable fashion! Had you no concern at all for my feelings?"

"But of course," Nick shrugged. "Believe me, I was most concerned about that unruly temper of yours, which might have spoilt everything. You really should learn to control it, you know."

Amanda drew an angry breath. "Well, I'd far rather have a temper than be a great cold fish like you, with no human emotions at all!"

"Is that so?" Nick's pale eyes glittered with sudden anger. Without warning, he jerked her hard against his chest, and covered her mouth in a fierce, almost brutal kiss. The world spun dizzyingly as the searing contact lengthened, until with equal abruptness she was released. "There, was that cold enough for you?" he ground out, turning her shoulders around so that she faced forward once more. He then urged his horse into motion, not waiting for a reply.

Amanda stared blindly at the road ahead, aware of the tumultuous pounding of her heart. By all rights, she ought to have felt frightened, but instead she felt only a shortness of breath, and an enervating warmth spreading slowly through her body. Even though Nick's kiss was no more than a gesture of anger, it had somehow turned everything upside down. Nick had certainly demonstrated that despite his icily controlled demeanor, he was capable of an uncontrolled passion. And what was worse, Amanda could no longer pretend to herself that she did not find him perilously attractive.

From that moment on, a new constraint seemed to hang heavily between Nick and Amanda, and for the rest of that long ride not a single word was spoken. It was therefore with a marked degree of mutual relief that they finally arrived at Newhaven, shortly after two o'clock.

Having deposited Amanda in the waiting room of the coastal shipping office, Nick soon departed in search of a buyer for his horse. At first, Amanda felt grateful to be left to her own devices, free of the strain of Nick's presence; as the minutes slowly stretched into an hour, however, she began to fidget with anxiety. Finally, she abandoned the hard wooden bench, in favor of pacing the length of the room.

When Nick returned at last, the hard set of his features confirmed her suspicion that something had gone awry. "What is it, Nick?" she ventured to inquire. "Did you meet with some difficulty?"

His gray green eyes swept her coldly. "You needn't fear, Amanda, I've got the money for our passage. But your sister's pearls were paste, and I've had to sell my favorite mount for the princely sum of thirty guineas. I suppose I oughtn't mind the fact that I paid four hundred for him just last year."

Amanda started in surprise, not so much at the injustice as at the exorbitant price named. She refrained, however, from blurting out any criticism of such extravagance; experience was fast teaching her that it was better to guard her tongue where Nick was concerned. "Surely you'll be able to buy him back later?" she ventured.

"Perhaps so," he replied in clipped tones. "The fellow swore to hold him safe, but there's no saying he'll keep his word." Half closing his eyes, Nick reached up to massage his neck, and his coat stretched tight over his broad shoulders. "It couldn't be helped, I suppose, but I only pray that Darius isn't sold to some cowhanded squire who'd wreck his mouth before the end of the week."

The concern in his voice was very nearly palpable, and for a moment Amanda sensed a sincerity, almost even a vulnerability, that promptly made her forget her wariness. She took a step towards him, and gently touched his shoulder. "Nick, I'm sorry, really I am. Is there nothing I could do to help?"

He stiffened and looked down, but instead of responding to her sympathetic impulse, his eyes impaled her with a look of utter contempt. "What do you suggest? Selling yourself for a few extra guineas?"

She jerked away her hand as if it had been scalded and turned away, but not before he had seen the look of hurt upon her expressive face. She moved mechanically towards the window, staring out at the ocean as she fought to hold back foolish tears. Of course he hadn't wished to take her with him, and had only done so out of some long-forgotten sense of chivalry. But she had not realized how much he resented and despised her, and the knowledge was almost too much to bear. She did not quite know why it should hurt so much.

"Damn it, Amanda, I shouldn't have said that.

Look at me." Nick's voice came from behind her, and quite surprisingly, his tone was almost gentle. Unwillingly she turned, blinking back her tears and lifting her chin; she might be obliged to endure his scorn, but she would not take his pity.

"Well, Amanda, you've no shortage of pride, have you? Very well, I most humbly beg your pardon. After all," he added wearily, "I realize it's not your fault that you've gotten me into this mess."

Her hurt vanished in a sudden rush of temper. "*I've* gotten you into this?" she exclaimed, her fingers clenching into fists. "Pray tell me who was gambling away his inheritance at three o'clock in the morning? Who killed a man? Who abducted and ruined whom? Who—"

Nick clamped a large hand over her mouth, casting a hasty glance around the room. When he saw that the window was firmly closed, however, and there was no fear of Amanda having been overheard by some passerby, he slowly released her.

"Your point is well taken," he admitted. "But would you mind saving this litany of my sins for a less public place? Besides, you give me too much credit." His smile took on a cruel twist. "Much as I would have enjoyed ruining you, you'd already accomplished that yourself." She could not help but flinch at the words, as she was forced to acknowledge their painful accuracy.

"Now let's make one thing clear, Amanda," he continued. "I'm not particularly proud of my own behavior yesterday, and I'm doing my damnedest to make amends. But nor am I accustomed to caring for the feelings of anyone by myself, and I warn you, don't push me too far with that sharp tongue of yours. Believe me, I don't relish the role of Good Samaritan, and it won't take much for me to change my mind and be damned to you. Do you understand?"

She managed to nod.

"Very well, then," he continued. "I'll be off now to book our passage. I suggest you sit here quietly until I return; it seems an unlikely place for you to cause me any more mischief." He then turned on his heel and stalked out.

Amanda watched him depart with a mixture of irritation and relief. His arrogance was simply astounding; she scarcely knew whether he had just uttered an apology or an accusation. Was he too lacking in moral feeling to realize that he was in the wrong, or was he simply too selfish to be concerned? Still, he had seemed quite human for that one brief moment, and despite his harshness toward her, he had not yet withdrawn his offer of protection. If only she could prevent herself from arousing that devil in him!

The office was located only a few steps away from the pier, and from where she sat, next to the window, she could see the Channel itself. The sky was bright, with large clouds which occasionally obscured the sun, and the wind was brisk, judging from the small white crests upon the waves. Amanda, who had never been upon the waves before, resolved that she would be an excellent sailor; Nick would no doubt expect her to succumb to *mal de mer*, and she would take enormous pleasure in proving him wrong.

Only a scant quarter of an hour had passed when the door opened. Amanda rose to greet Nick, but it was not he who sauntered in; instead it was a middle-aged gentleman of medium height and swarthy complexion. He was dressed in an extreme of fashion which she had never seen before, from his pale yellow pantaloons to the absurd height of his shirt points, preventing him from turning his head more than a few inches in either side. His waistcoat was festooned with dangling chains and watch fobs, and Amanda could count over ten capes attached to his great-coat. She was not well acquainted with dandies, but instinctively her own good taste was repelled by such ostentation.

Hastily she averted her eyes from this spectacle, but not before he had raised his quizzing glass, his hand glittering with rings. She was uncomfortably aware of being inspected from head to toe, although dignity prevented her from objecting aloud.

"Where's your mistress, sweetheart?" he inquired unctuously, sweeping off his tall beaver hat as he strolled closer. Amanda's heart sank as she realized that once again she was to be mistaken for a governess or an abigail.

"Are you bound for France?" the man pursued, and Amanda felt impelled to respond with a brief nod. "Tongue-tied, eh? That's good—I fancy the shy ones!" He laughed gratingly. "I'm off to Paris, myself, and I wouldn't mind a bit of companionship on the journey. How'd you like to double your salary, m'dear?"

The man leaned close suddenly, and Amanda could smell wine upon his breath. "I find you offensive, sir," she snapped, unable to hold her tongue a moment longer. "Pray leave me alone!"

"That's the way, sweetheart," he chuckled. "They always say no, and they always mean yes! Come now, we'll have a lovely time, and at journey's end, I'll make sure you're well taken care of. What d'you say to a few new dresses, or even a bauble or two? Just the thing for that pretty neck of yours."

He reached out a hairy hand and seized hold of her chin, ignoring her gasp of revulsion. She tried to twist out of his grasp, but he merely pulled her closer, and she was horrified to see a blaze of desire in his eyes. "You're too pretty for an abigail," he murmured. "Someone should have taken care of you long ago."

"Amanda, I—" Nick strode into the room, and momentarily froze on the doorstep. In a split second he had taken in the scene, and his face hardened. "Let her go," he commanded softly.

The stranger involuntarily dropped his hand and stepped backwards, but then he narrowed his eyes, glancing back and forth between Nick and Amanda. Then he smiled unpleasantly. "I see. Someone has indeed taken care of you. But my offer still stands, my dear. Double your current allowance."

Two long strides forward, and then Nick's fist connected with the man's jaw, sending him spinning into a tumbled heap upon the floor. The man lay panting for a moment, and then heaved himself up on one elbow, shrinking back as he saw Nick's tall form looming with menace above him.

"I say, I beg your pardon!" he apologized hurriedly. "I didn't know she was your wife!"

"She's not," Nick denied irritably.

"But then—?" The man's eyes widened in surprise. Nick looked at him with disgusted comprehension, and then glanced swiftly at Amanda's unconsciously pleading expression.

"She happens to be my sister," Nick bit out reluctantly. "Now get out of here unless you want another taste of my home-brewed!"

The man struggled to his feet and hastily retreated, pausing only to scoop up his dust-streaked hat before slamming the door behind him.

Amanda heard herself utter a sigh of relief, and realized that she had been holding her breath until that very moment. She raised her eyes to Nick's face.

"Thank you," she gasped with heartfelt sincerity. "I never thought I would ever be so grateful to see you."

Nick did not reply immediately, and she could see that the tautness had not left his expression. "Were you indeed grateful? I acted without thinking, and perhaps I should apologize for having interrupted you."

"What on earth do you mean?" she exclaimed in bewilderment.

"You seemed to be on such excellent terms with that fellow that anyone might think you were trying to better your circumstances; after all, my pockets are sadly to let at the moment." He motioned towards the door. "Shall I call him back for you?"

Amanda paled, and then flushed as she comprehended his meaning. "How *dare* you insinuate such a contemptible thing!" she flung at him. "Must you judge everyone by your own low standards of behaviour?"

"I've never known a woman who did not have her price," he shrugged dismissively. "For a share of a fat roll of banknotes or the promise of a few diamonds, more than a few would welcome such attentions. And I don't speak of doxies, my girl; it's the married ladies of the highest rank who put your sex to the blush."

Amanda seethed, but before she could think of a suitably crushing retort, loud shouts from outside recalled them both to their surroundings, and to the imminent departure of the ship. After a final exchange of glares, Nick turned on his heel and Amanda followed him silently out of the room. As they boarded the ship, however, she found herself wondering about the strangeness of his reaction to the incident. No matter what were his cynical views of women, surely he did not believe that she had actually invited the advances of that odious man. If it were anyone else, one might suppose his unreasonable response to have been inspired by jealousy—but of course, that notion was ludicrous.

At the same time, nevertheless, she had to admit that her knowledge of the sophisticated world was far less than his. Perhaps he was right, and ladies of society did behave in such a scandalous manner. But even so, he had no right to suppose that even in the horrid circumstances to which she had been reduced, she would ever consider for one moment the kind of conduct he seemed to take for granted. Not all women were cast in the same mold, and she would prove to him somehow how very wrong he was about her.

There was only a handful of other passengers embarking, and within a short time the gangplank was hauled in and the anchor weighed. Amanda chose to remain on deck, partly from curiosity at the sailors' bustling activity, and partly from the cowardly desire to avoid the unpleasant stranger. It was also a relief to be free of Nick's brooding silence, even for a short while.

The air on deck was much colder than Amanda had anticipated, as clouds drifted across the blue of the sky. A brisk wind whipped her skirts about her ankles, and loosened her tawny hair from its neatly-coiled chignon. She brushed the strands out of her eyes and watched the receding shoreline, clutching the railing as the ship bobbed up and down in the choppy waters. Little by little she could feel her anxieties ebbing away, dwarfed by the wild grandeur of the ocean. Amanda had never travelled to the Continent before, and the very idea of Paris lifted her spirits immeasurably. For a moment she allowed herself to indulge in fantasy, closing her eyes and imagining a glittering salon, with herself reigning supreme at its center, acclaimed for her beauty, wit, and exquisite clothes . . .

"You seem to have taken well to the sea." At the sound of a voice, Amanda started and opened her eyes, to find Nick leaning on the rail only a few paces away. His pale hair was ruffled by the wind, and his eyes were a deep green, reflecting the color of the waves. The angles of his face were sharply defined in the afternoon sun, and suddenly it struck Amanda that despite his quixotic and infuriating temperament, he was undoubtedly the most handsome man she had ever seen. And not merely handsome, it was even more than that. There was a certain magnetism about him which made it impossible to even notice the presence of any other man. She ruefully acknowledged to herself that an unsuspecting female might drown in the everchanging depths of those eyes—and no doubt many had.

She would not find herself among them, however, and in any case, if they were to travel together, it was vital to establish some basis of mutual trust. They would simply have to deal with that regrettable encounter in the waiting room.

"Nick, we must talk," she declared firmly. "You never gave me a chance to explain what happened with that man."

His expression became cold and remote. "You needn't bother to fabricate a tale, my dear. I cut my eyeteeth years ago."

Amanda made a little sound of frustration. "It was not as you think. I had done my best to discourage him, but—"

"So much so that I found you practically in his arms," he replied sardonically.

"Oh, very well, then!" Amanda exclaimed, losing the last thread of her patience. "Think what you please! It's quite obvious that you're determined to believe the worst no matter what I say. But I did *not* encourage that man, and in another moment I would have landed him a facer myself!"

He gave a contemptuous snort which left no doubt of his opinion of her fighting abilities. "That's as may be. But at least I begin to believe the tale of your hoydenish upbringing, with that charming bit of boxing cant!"

Amanda could feel her cheeks grow hot. "If you find my speech offensive, sir, you are welcome to relieve yourself of my lowering company. I would as lief be alone, as be subjected to constant criticism!"

"Well, well," he drawled. "Now that's the first time we've ever been entirely in agreement. I don't suppose you have any practical suggestions as to how we may bring about a parting of our ways?"

She shook her head, and the sunlight glinting off the soft waves of her hair drew Nick's unwilling attention for a moment, before his ill-humored gaze returned to her face. "I'm afraid I haven't any ideas. I did have a school friend years ago named Celia Thornton, who married a French baron whose name I don't recall. They were living in London at the time, but perhaps they might have returned to Paris now that the war is over, and I could try to locate them and enlist their aid."

"You may as well try to find the man in the moon, if Paris is still the Bedlam it was a few months ago."

"How would you know?" she inquired curiously. "Have you been there since the Armistice?"

"Oh, yes," he replied, and there was a tinge of bitterness in his voice. "I was in Paris last fall, when the *émigrés* flocked back on the coattails of the new Louis. It was a riotous time, I assure you. But I was scarcely there to confer with Talleyrand; there were too many fêtes to attend, and too many bottles to be drunk."

Amanda's brows drew together in puzzled concern. It was obvious that something was wrong with Nick's account; why did he behave so disgracefully, if he felt disgust for that sort of life?

"Did you fight in the War?" she ventured.

"I served in the Life Guards for six months."

"Only six months?" She could not prevent her exclamation. "Were you invalided out?"

"Hardly." The single word was weighted with scorn. "My father died, and the blasted trustees forced me to sell out. Lord knows I didn't want to, but his will was tied up so neatly that I couldn't get round it. So while my friends were saving the world from Boney, I was adorning the bow window at White's." He smiled grimly. "Of course, I did risk my neck quite often, if one considers the curricle racing."

Amanda had a sudden vision of Nick as a fervent idealistic young soldier, barred from the field of honor and shamed by his enforced leisure. No wonder he had plunged into a life of pleasure-seeking; as long as he could not fight, nothing else would have mattered a scrap.

"You asked about Paris," he continued in a

carefully neutral voice. "From what I saw of it, the city is struggling back to life. The treasuries were exhausted by Boney's troops, of course, but now that trade has resumed . . ."

Amanda listened attentively, aware that Nick was not interested in polite conversation, but was rather shutting his mind against painful memories. Nevertheless, there seemed to be a new harmony between them, as though he himself had wearied of their mutual antagonism. Amanda did her best to prolong this delicate new mood by asking questions, and little by little he allowed himself to be drawn out.

His descriptions of travel upon the Continent were lively and humorous, and from time to time Amanda caught glimpses of intriguing depths of character lurking behind Nick's habitual nonchalance. Despite the superficiality of his preferred mode of existence, he did not lack for intelligence or understanding of his fellow man. Some of his anecdotes were rather warm, detailing adventures with expensive lightskirts, but while Amanda blushed, she maintained an admirable composure. The truce between them was too fragile to allow for outraged protests on her part, and besides, it was all really quite interesting!

Eventually the conversation turned to Nick's days at Oxford, a place which had fascinated Amanda ever since her tomboyish childhood. She pressed him for descriptions of the dons, the ceremonies, and the historic colleges that she had only seen depicted in books. Amanda even quizzed him about his tutorials, and when he protested that he had paid them as little attention as possible, she eyed him with marked disapproval.

"Really, Amanda, one would almost think you would have wished to go to Oxford yourself!" he mocked.

"I would have given anything to do so," she answered, quite seriously. "My father tutored me in Greek and Latin, and I was far better at it than my playfellows. In fact, they used to bribe me to do their compositions. Peter used to say—" She hesitated for a moment, and then continued calmly. "Peter used to say that had I been a man, I would have been either a famous don or a clergyman."

"Well, since you're quite obviously not a man," Nick gave a flickering glance at her feminine curves, "I advise you not to say this to your admirers. Gentlemen are usually put off by bluestockings, you know."

Amanda favored him with an affronted look. "I don't know why I ought to be ashamed of having a brain. And even if such were the case, you're scarcely one of my admirers, as you put it so charmingly."

"Most assuredly, I am not!" he agreed, but his exaggerated grimace of distaste humorously gave the lie to his words.

For an instant they regarded each other with something approaching a feeling of camaraderie, but then Nick seemed to withdraw into himself, as if too much had been revealed too soon. "It will be getting dark," he declared curtly. "We'd best get below, out of this wind."

Amanda shivered from a sudden chill. It was

almost as though Nick's good humor of the previous hours had been warming her physically. Now that that friendliness was gone, she wondered dispiritedly whether the fleeting sense of harmony would ever return.

After a restless sleep in her cramped private cabin, Amanda rose the next morning to watch the coast of France emerge from the mist in sharp relief. When Nick joined her at the rail some time later, she could not prevent an exclamation of pleasure as their port of destination came into view.

"You needn't wax so enthusiastic," he replied coolly. "Dieppe is noted more for its thievery than its hospitality. It's as well we have no baggage, because very likely someone would try to steal it." He continued on, ignoring her crestfallen look. "But don't worry, once we get to Paris, it will be worth the trouble. I can show you some places—" He broke off, as the ship's captain began shouting instructions and the sailors prepared to bring the ship into port.

Amanda watched the bustling activity with outward interest, but her thoughts were turning over Nick's careless words. He had mentioned showing her the city; did this mean that he was no longer anxious to be rid of her? At the notion, she felt flooded with a warm excitement, and then her heart gave a sudden lurch.

This was how it felt to be in love! She gripped the rail, not daring to look at him. This was it— the heightened senses, the awareness of his every movement, the hypnotic fascination produced by his look or by his voice. Once Peter had made her feel this way, but even as she clung to the memory of her old love, she realized that this was somehow different.

There was a sensual magnetism about Nick that Amanda had never encountered before. Five years ago, she would have been frightened, had she even been able to recognize it. Now, however, she was older, and the bitter hurts of the past had lent a new maturity to her feelings. Nick had the power to attract her physically, in a way that Peter never had.

But was this truly love? The very notion was ridiculous—after all, she had known him for little more than a few days! And besides, despite the depth of their conversation on the previous day, much of what she had seen in him was unpleasant. By her observation and by his own admission, he was a gamester who had killed his man in a duel, and a self-centered libertine who would stop at little to satisfy his whims. How could she, who had loved a gentle caring boy like Peter, ever stoop to the level of a creature like Nick?

Even as the question crossed her mind, however, the answer was painfully obvious. Nick was not a boy, but a man. And a dynamic, vitally attractive man at that, whose quick wits had kept her continually off balance. To Amanda, whose life had for years been deprived of physical affection and intellectual companionship, the combination was a dangerous one.

The only thing she could be thankful for was that he had not appeared to take any real notice of her as a woman. His chivalrous gesture of bringing her to France, for example, had been motivated by the sort of pity he might have felt for a runaway child; if she became troublesome, it was likely that he would wash his hands of her entirely. Even his kiss during their escape from that horrid inn had been impersonal, an act of revenge for his affronted pride, rather than a betrayal of desire. And that was no doubt a blessing, Amanda confessed to herself, because if Nick ever decided to pursue her in earnest, she knew that it might take every ounce of courage she possessed to withstand him.

Chapter Four

As the small ship hauled into port, Amanda saw
that the dock area was smaller than she had presumed. The trade which had been interrupted
during the long hostilities between England and
France had resumed with a vengeance, but there
was evidence of neglect in the decrepit condition of
the docks and the rundown appearance of the
warehouses that lined the quayside. Amid the
groups of shouting sailors and tradesmen, however, there were a few well-dressed onlookers,
waiting to greet the passengers as they disem-
barked.

Amanda and Nick, having no baggage, were the
first ones off the boat, but before they could take
stock of their surroundings, a high-pitched female
voice came floating across to where they stood.

"Sir Nicholas! Oh, Sir Nicholas!" Amanda
watched in surprise as a woman detached herself
from the crowd and moved forward to greet them.
At that moment, Nick had automatically taken

Amanda's arm to help her over the uneven gangway, and Amanda caught a brief look of disdainful inquiry upon the woman's face. It was gone in a flash, however, as the woman addressed Nick in a silky accented voice.

"Dear Sir Nicholas, it is a happiness so great to see you again! I did not know you were coming to France—you should have written!" She placed a hand upon his arm and smiled up at him coquettishly.

"Liliane! What the devil are you doing here?" he exclaimed half-irritably.

"I am here to receive a shipment of lace from Holland—of the most beautiful, I assure you, and no one in Paris has seen it yet! I must have it for the ball of Madame la Duchesse de Renard next week. You will be there, yes?"

Completely ignored, Amanda had ample opportunity to study the woman at leisure. She was dressed expensively in a manner which Amanda supposed to be the height of fashion; her full curves were molded by a red silk pelisse, which despite the chilly air revealed a near-transparent muslin gown draped quite low across the bosom. Her gleaming auburn hair was only partly concealed by a modish hat, trimmed with swaying ostrich plumes that framed her pale skin and flashing dark brown eyes to perfection. A sharp-eyed, middle-aged abigail hovered discreetly behind her, and a lackey stood at the ready, carrying a small portmanteau for the awaited parcel.

Amanda was not vain, but she could not help

suffering a twinge of humiliation at her own dowdy appearance. She had long been resigned to seeing Chloe showered with new gowns, while she herself made do with an occasional new sash and skillful mending. Living in the isolation of the country, however, there had been little contact with fashionable society. Now she could see exactly why women of the *ton* were said to lavish whole fortunes upon their backs: a stunning example stood here before her very eyes. Amanda was not Miss Waverley for nothing, however, and she managed to conceal her embarrassment behind an air of cool composure.

The woman chatted on to Nick, obviously treating him as something more than an old friend. She was behaving as though the younger woman did not exist, and much to Amanda's chagrin, Nick appeared equally oblivious. Amanda also realized with a start that the woman had addressed Nick as "Sir Nicholas"; with all that had happened in such a short time, it seemed incredible that she still did not know her companion's identity!

At that moment, Nick's elbow was jostled by the obnoxious dandy they had encountered earlier. "I beg your pardon, sir," he exclaimed, eyeing Nick warily. "And a thousand apologies for our little confusion earlier, eh? A pleasant journey, sir, to you and to your lovely sister." Executing a small bow, the man hurried away.

His words had a startling effect upon all three persons standing there. Amanda flushed, remembering that embarrassing incident; the woman cocked her head and slowly turned to assess Amanda with new eyes; and Nick glared at Amanda as though he would have liked to tear her limb from limb.

"So this is your sister? How she is pretty! You must introduce us, Sir Nicholas." This patently insincere praise was delivered in a warmer tone than Amanda might have anticipated; it was obvious that the lady was not one to appreciate the charms of her rivals, but that a sister might be accorded a bit of friendly condescension.

Nick obliged unwillingly. "Amanda, may I present Madame Liliane Demorest. Liliane, my—" he choked slightly, "my sister, Amanda."

"Miss Malvern, what a pleasure to make your acquaintance," the woman replied with perfunctory courtesy. Amanda blinked at being newly christened in this fashion, managing only a polite nod of response. There was no need to make further conversation, however, as Madame Demorest turned her attention immediately back to Nick.

"Whatever is she doing here with you, Sir Nicholas?" she asked curiously, darting a meaningful glance at Amanda's shabby apparel.

"We're here on holiday," Nick replied grimly, looking as if a pleasant vacation were the furthest thing from his mind. Following Madame Demorest's disparaging gaze, he realized that further embroidery was necessary. "She's my half sister, actually; been living in the country, and I've brought her along to give her a bit of town bronze." His eyes swept critically over Amanda's windblown hair and blooming complexion, and he decided to add a final fillip. "Of course, she hasn't yet made her comeout at home."

Madame Demorest was only half listening, and she accepted this explanation without comment, but Amanda's mouth nearly fell open in surprise. Not out yet—why, that would put her at sixteen or seventeen years of age! She hardly knew whether to be complimented or insulted; knowing Nick, she was inclined towards the latter.

"That is nothing! You shall get her some proper clothes, and I shall get her a fine French husband," Madame Demorest assured. "And then we will have time for ourselves, no?"

Amanda could not refrain from bobbing a small ironic curtsey. "Thank you, Madame, you are very kind," she responded in what she hoped was a schoolgirlish voice, while Nick uttered a muffled cough.

"Tell me, Sir Nicholas," Madame Demorest continued, moving closer and smiling flirtatiously up into his face. "Where are you staying in Paris? I do so much wish to see more of you."

"We'll be stopping with the Comtesse de Richelet," Nick answered. "But what about Jules?"

"In Austria again. Alas, the life of a diplomat!" Her voice dropped to an intimate whisper. "So I am quite alone. May I hope for a visit soon?"

Nick's eyes gleamed with understanding. Bowing low over Madame Demorest's hand, he pressed a light kiss upon it. "Of course," he murmured.

69

"And you must bring your delightful sister to see me sometime, too," she added perfunctorily.

"Oh, thank you, Madame," Amanda breathed, inwardly furious at the woman's insulting air of superiority, not to mention Nick's disgustingly obvious admiration of her charms. "You are so kind, and I do think you are so much prettier than Nicky's other lady friends!" Amanda smiled artlessly, relishing the woman's look of discomfiture.

"Sorry, we must be off," Nick announced hastily, and seizing Amanda's arm he dragged her off toward the row of vehicles for hire. It was not until they were bundled into a closed carriage, safely out of earshot, that he rounded upon her.

"I should thrash you for that piece of impertinence, you little vixen!" he exclaimed angrily.

"What else do you expect from a schoolroom miss?" she retorted. "Besides, it nearly made me sick to see her hanging upon you like that. She might as well have asked you to pack a nightshirt when you come to visit!"

Nick's lips curled in a slightly sardonic smile. "As a matter of fact, I don't generally need a nightshirt on such occasions."

Amanda flushed, hastily changing the subject. "In any case, it was your fault for making me out to be a child. How could you suggest something so utterly ridiculous?"

Nick frowned. "Damn it, I had to say something after that fool called you my sister. I couldn't very well call him a liar, not after I'd knocked him down for it. Besides, I didn't want Liliane to think that you were my mistress."

"Why not?" Amanda's voice was very cool. "You wished to protect my reputation, or you didn't wish to make her jealous?"

"Don't be a fool," he reproved. "If anyone thought I dressed my mistresses as shabbily as that, I'd never live it down."

There was an outraged gasp. "Pray forgive me for embarrassing you," she murmured with unconcealed sarcasm.

"Well, I suppose it wasn't your fault," he allowed charitably. "But the worst of it is, we'll have to follow through on this charade, at least until I can think of a way to be rid of you."

"Don't put yourself to the trouble," Amanda snapped. "I can arrange for my own disappearance, thank you." All he wanted was to be free of her burdensome presence: very well, she would find a way to oblige him. No doubt there was some form of honest employment she could secure! Amanda was suddenly horrified to feel tears pricking at her eyelids; whatever on earth was the matter with her?

"Oh no, you don't, my girl," he warned. "Your sudden disappearance now would set too many tongues wagging, and another scandal is something I can very well do without. Now, be quiet and let me think of a plan of action." He stretched out his long limbs, linking his arms behind his head, and frowned at nothing in particular.

On the opposite seat, Amanda folded her arms defiantly and stared blindly out of the carriage

71

window. How dare he act as though all that mattered was his own reputation, forcing her into such an impossibly awkward situation! More than ever, it seemed imperative to leave his company, and Amanda resolved that no matter how slim a hope it may be, she would try to locate her friend Celia at the earliest opportunity.

It was nearly dawn of the following day when the carriage drew to a halt in front of a large town house that was their apparent destination. Amanda would have vastly preferred to break their journey, but their funds were now so low that they could barely afford the necessary change of horses and a hastily-swallowed cup of chocolate every few hours. She was too exhausted to take any notice as Nick roused a sleepy-eyed servant and had a brief conversation that seemed to satisfy the man's curiosity. They were shown to two rooms abovestairs, and Amanda did no more than shed her clothes before collapsing into bed.

Not until late afternoon did she awaken and take stock of her surroundings. The bedroom in which she found herself was elegantly furnished with delicate gilt furniture, and the walls were hung with flocked red silk; whoever owned this place had excellent if not lavish taste. The canopied four-poster in which she lay was more comfortable than any she had ever enjoyed, and she yawned and stretched with lazy contentment. It was not the moment, however, to go back to sleep, no matter how inviting that prospect. Far more important was the need to discover exactly where she was, and what schemes lay in store for her future.

The first step was to wash and dress, but her gown was not to be found upon the chair over which it had been hastily draped. Wearing only her shift, Amanda threw back the bedcovers and went to open the door of the large ornate wardrobe, supposing a maid to have hung it there. Only emptiness greeted her, and she was about to close the door when the sound of a doorknob turning startled her from behind. Hastily she stepped back, instinctively using the wardrobe door as a shield, so that only her bare feet and slender ankles could be seen as she peered around its edge.

It was not a maid who entered, however, but Nick.

"Good morning, Amanda," he said cheerfully, sauntering into the room. "I trust that you slept well."

"Yes, thank you. Have you forgotten how to knock?" she replied frostily. "And would you be good enough to tell me what has happened to my clothes?"

"They're getting a good clean and brush—something you could rather do with yourself," he added unkindly.

She reddened, only too aware of her disheveled state.

"I'll ask the maid to bring you one of *Tante* Sophie's dressing gowns. The servants have told me she's out of town at the moment, but she'll be back within a day or so."

"Who on earth is *Tante* Sophie?" Amanda inquired, still hanging on to the wardrobe door as though it were a shield.

"The Comtesse de Richelet, my aunt by marriage," Nick informed her. "It's a distant connection, and she's never taken much interest in my branch of the family, but she allows me to stay here when I'm in Paris. Something about my rapskallion charm, she says." The corner of his mouth curved in a self-deprecating smile, and Amanda blinked. She could certainly see what *Tante* Sophie meant! "Her son, my cousin Louis, is a good friend of mine, you'll meet him as well. Now, this is the important part: I've never mentioned a sister before, but as I say, the connection is distant, and I don't believe they'll be inquiring too closely. You'll continue as my young half sister, and we'll call Louis your cousin as well; that should satisfy the gossips."

"And then what?" Amanda had to ask. "Can you help me to find Celia?"

He shook his head dismissively. "Too late for that now. Even if you found your erstwhile friend, the Baroness, there's no saying she'd wish to acknowledge you. And by now Liliane Demorest has no doubt spread the word that my sister is here. All in all, it looks as though we'll have to carry on with this charade.

"What I've decided is this. I'll get you some proper clothes, and take you round a bit socially. Then, after a decent interval has passed, I'll simply arrange for you to be married."

74

"Married?" The door swung alarmingly. "You must be mad!"

"It's the only way out of this coil," Nick insisted firmly. "It's now too late for you to vanish into thin air. And even if you should try, you know as well as I that your choice is between some form of lowly employment and living under someone's protection. Needless to say, neither alternative would look at all well if you should be found out."

"Your only concern being your own reputation, of course!" Amanda bristled.

"No, not entirely," was his unexpected reply. "I believe that marriage is the best answer to your needs, Amanda. You'll have security and money, which is enough to satisfy any female. We'll have to concoct some story about your lack of dowry, but even without one, my name should be good enough to attract any number of suitors. All in all, you ought to consider yourself quite fortunate."

"I certainly do not!" Amanda countered indignantly. "And I will not sell myself in such a fashion, all for the sake of your good name! It may interest you to know that I don't give two pins for your good name, whatever it may happen to be!"

An angry glint came into Nick's green eyes, and his mouth hardened. "Don't bore me with a display of outraged virtue, Amanda," he said, in the silky tone she had already learned to beware. "And you may not care for my reputation, but I most assuredly do. The name of Malvern is one which you will honor, like it or not."

"You can't force me!" Amanda said defiantly.

"Can't I just?" he riposted. "You'll do as I say, wherever and whenever I say. Or would you rather I throw you out of this house, right now, and be damned to you?"

There was a dreadful silence as Amanda recalled the momentary helplessness of her position. She had no choice but to shake her head mutely.

"Well, then," he said, his manner thawing slightly. "I knew you'd see reason. I assure you, this charade is an accursed nuisance all round, and for both our sakes I'll be glad when this is over." He turned and headed toward the door, glancing back when his hand was upon the knob. "And don't imagine that you can cross swords with me, Amanda. I'm known to be a rather deadly opponent." The door slammed shut behind him with ominous decision.

In the mirror above the washbasin, Amanda saw her own face reflected, the color in her cheeks heightened and her golden eyes wide and darkened with apprehension. And not only with apprehension, but with something else which she dared not name to herself, a shiver of excitement which Nick's presence had aroused, and which even his callous anger had not banished.

As she performed the necessary ablutions, she mused that it would not be easy to defy Nick, although, of course, she had no intention of falling in with his plans. He was entirely selfish, and argument would serve only to provoke the kind of unreasonable temper she had just witnessed. The safest course of action, she determined

76

to herself, would be to comply outwardly with his wishes, until an opportunity for escape should present itself, as it surely must.

A shy housemaid named Martine soon brought Amanda's dress, which no amount of brushing could have made into a presentable garment. There was no choice but to put it back on, however, and when she made her way downstairs a short while later, she found Nick waiting for her in the salon. It was a lovely room which again betokened sophisticated taste; there were lemon-colored sofas with delicately carved legs and rolled arms, resting upon large Aubusson carpets. Mirrors topped the ornate fireplace, which was carved into linen folds and tassels. And everywhere she looked, there was the gleam of gilt and the smooth reflectiveness of glass and marble. This modish decor was far removed from than that of the London town houses Amanda recalled from her brief season, not to mention the countrified simplicity of the Waverley manor.

"Your aunt is fortunate to own such a beautiful house," Amanda observed, but as he rose to his feet Nick replied with lazy cynicism. "No need to mince words—you mean she's rich. Oh, yes, *Tante* Sophie is swimming in lard. The family lost everything except their heads in the Terror, but young Louis has made it up and more. He's the cleverest gamester I've ever known, as well as a complete hand with the ladies."

"Your cousin sounds quite charming," Amanda said drily. Another womanizing card player was hardly a pleasing prospect! "When shall I have the privilege of meeting him?"

"I don't know," Nick shrugged. "As I told you, they're not here; if his mother hasn't made him accompany her on her little jaunt, he may return at any moment. If he does show up, though, it won't do to let him know the truth about you. He's a good fellow, but not to be trusted with such a secret.

"In the meantime," Nick continued, "there are a few practicalities to be considered. First of all, I've got to reline my pockets, and Foley's Bank has a branch here that should advance me whatever I need on account; my family has dealt with them for years. Then, our next priority must be to get you some decent clothes. No one would believe you to be my sister in that shabby rig. Do you wish to come along, or shall I kit you out myself and have it all sent back to the house?"

Amanda had little doubt of Nick's familiarity with feminine apparel, and the very notion of his selecting her garments was too disturbing to contemplate. "Thank you, but I prefer to accompany you," she said with a touch of primness. "On the understanding, of course, that whatever you spend on my behalf shall be repaid in full as soon as I can manage."

"Of course," Nick agreed, although the ironic light in his eyes would—had Amanda noticed it— have revealed to her his opinion of such a likelihood. Within his experience, the fair sex was not adept at keeping accounts, at least when someone else was footing the bills!

After waiting for Amanda to procure her cloak, he led her outside to the curb, where a perch phaeton was standing at the ready, a groom holding the horse's head. A few minutes later, they were proceeding at a brisk trot through the narrow streets of Paris. Amanda had to admit that Nick was a highly skilled whip, as he controlled the horses with a light but sure touch. It was also a pleasure to ride in such a modern, well-sprung vehicle, a far cry from the cumbersome carriages preferred by Lady Ruth, and which Amanda never had been permitted to drive herself. Her heart lightened, and though her situation must still be viewed with some trepidation, it would have been impossible to deny that comfortable surroundings and new clothes would be a pleasing prospect.

After a short drive through winding cobbled streets, they arrived in a more congested business district, and pulled up before a large forbidding building of gray stone fronted by imposing columns.

"Foley's," Nick announced brusquely. He glanced around and scowled. "Hang it all, there's no one about to hold the beast, and he's not half-restless today."

"I can hold him for you," Amanda asserted calmly.

"You?" The single word was derisive.

"Yes, certainly!" she defended. "I'm not quite the imbecile you seem to think me. I have handled horses, and was even used to drive myself."

His answering look was quizzical. "You haven't the faintest notion of what I think of you, which is perhaps just as well. But you'll find that trotting a farm-bred cob down a country lane is not the same as controlling a horse of spirit. So be it, then, you may see if you can hold him." He handed her the reins and leaped down lightly. "All you need do is keep him still; I'll not be above ten minutes."

But it was more than half an hour before Nick reemerged through the door, still muttering curses. After being kept waiting forever by a bunch of damned clerks, they had had the temerity to demand proof of his identity! It had taken a good deal of argument before they would allow him to see the manager, who, after more delay, had finally accepted his credentials. And now, to cap off his irritation, he discovered that the phaeton was nowhere in sight.

He stood fuming for a long moment, but before he could make up his mind what to do next, the vehicle in question came rumbling around the corner, with Amanda at the ribbons. She pulled the horse up short, directly in front of Nick, and he saw with grudging respect that she caught the thong of the whip with graceful expertise.

"Where the devil have you been?" he exclaimed, not permitting any admiration to show as he climbed back up to the seat. "I ought to give you a good tanning for risking your neck and Louis's prize gelding in this city traffic!"

"Oh no, pray don't!" Amanda replied cheerfully. "You took such a long time that I feared the horse might catch a chill. I simply took a little drive as far as the Town Hall."

"You went all that way alone? How did you know to get there?" Nick demanded incredulously.

"I asked directions, of course."

He cast her a sidelong glance. "You found someone who spoke English, then."

"Not at all, I spoke French. You needn't look so surprised; there are all manner of things I can do, and some better than you, I don't doubt."

Nick flicked the reins, setting the horses back into motion. "I'm very certain that there are," he agreed, but somehow his tone was not at all complimentary. "And now, if you don't mind, we should proceed to the next order of business."

The rest of the afternoon was to be devoted to the transformation of Miss Amanda Waverley, dowdy spinster, into Miss Amanda Malvern, a wealthy young lady not yet formally out in society. At first the lady in question objected strenuously to the latter aspect of that role, protesting that it was a far cry from twenty-three to seventeen. Nick, on the other hand, insisted that with the appropriately youthful clothing and a tight rein on her behavior—which he intended to supervise with the strictest care—the masquerade would succeed. Ruthlessly overruled, Amanda resigned herself to the demeaning role.

After a time, however, she could not resist the pleasantly heady sensation of entering shops which were far more exclusive than any she had ever imagined, and being treated as a preferred customer. She observed wryly that Nick was recognized and greeting with fawning warmth in some of the shops they visited, all modistes of the first stare. She could only surmise that he treated his mistresses as well as he had earlier claimed. But she was far from being the guardian of his morals, and she bit back the caustic comments that hovered on her lips.

There was also no doubt that she was benefitting from his expertise, no matter how improperly acquired. Although the lingering effects of the war still resulted in some shortages of dry goods, the quality of the French workmanship was exquisite, and Amanda had never seen such beautiful clothes. Nick took full control, conferring with the modiste over patterns and fabrics while Amanda stood to one side, idly fingering the bolts of delicate cloth. From time to time she would have liked to assert her own judgment, but she had to admit that his taste was excellent, and that he was far more conversant with current fashion than she.

Only once did he pay any attention to her preferences, and that was when he noticed her gazing at a made-up gown hanging up for display. It was of fine, cream-colored muslin, shot through with glimmering golden threads, and draped into a gown with tiny puffed sleeves and a modestly curved neckline. It was gathered simply under the bodice with bronze ribbons, falling in Grecian folds. Amanda sighed unconsciously, tracing her slender fingers over the shimmering fabric.

The modiste approached, scenting another sale.

"Ah, that one," she approved. "It will suit mademoiselle to perfection. And the model is almost her exact size—would mademoiselle care to try it on?"

Startled, Amanda glanced uncertainly at Nick, and he nodded curtly. "You need at least one gown to wear immediately," he conceded. "That one might be suitable."

Amanda followed the modiste into a dressing room where skillful hands soon helped her out of her shabby gown. The woman clucked disapprovingly at the sight of Amanda's threadbare undergarments, and she left the room briefly, to reappear only a moment later with an armload of shifts and stockings. Amanda soon found herself clad in new garments of softest silk, trimmed with delicate lace. Then the new gown was eased over her head, and Amanda had to stand patiently while the modiste inserted a few strategically placed stitches.

"Now we will show the dress to milord your brother, *n'est-ce pas?* But first . . ." The woman scrutinized Amanda's face, pursing her lips. "If mademoiselle will permit me to arrange the hair?" Amanda watched in amazement as her long hair was expertly brushed and pinned into a flattering upswept style, much less severe than her accustomed style of a modest chignon at the nape of her neck. The dressing room mirror now reflected a sophisticated young lady of fashion whom Amanda could hardly recognize as herself.

When she emerged, there was a long moment of silence as Nick's eyes scanned her figure from head to toe and back again. The new hairstyle and gown had worked a magical transformation, illuminating the creamy smoothness of Amanda's skin and setting off the golden sheen of her hair and topaz eyes to perfection. Amanda felt breathless as she waited for Nick's approval; his face was impassive, but his green eyes glowed with a strange intensity.

"Your sister, she is beautiful, *n'est-ce pas?*" the modiste prompted.

After a pause, Nick gave only the briefest of nods, but the simple gesture brought a rush of color to Amanda's cheeks, and for a moment their eyes locked. Then Amanda dropped her gaze hurriedly, afraid of what she might inadvertently reveal.

"You shouldn't be spending so much on me, Nick," she protested in a whisper, after an expensive Norwich silk shawl had been added to the pile of purchases. "You must know that I intend to repay you, but at this rate it will be quite impossible."

His pale brows lifted. "Come now, Amanda, no woman ever has enough clothes. And in any case, you needn't burden your conscience; you know quite well that this is intended more for my own benefit than for yours."

"Yes, but I cannot allow—"

"You what?" Nick said quite calmly. Under the curious eyes of the shopkeeper, he smiled at her, but in a way to send a shiver down her spine. "I beg you to recall our earlier discussion. I will be calling the shots, and I will have no arguments from my dearest little sister." But there was no trace of affection, brotherly or otherwise, in the none-too-gentle pat that he bestowed upon her cheek.

Amanda swallowed a retort; this was neither the time nor the place to get into another wrangle. She could not help but wonder, however, as he settled for their purchases, why it was that whenever she and Nick struck a common chord of understanding, he invariably withdrew. He did not seem to wish for any friendship to grow between them; rather, he seemed to prefer her in a subservient role, as though she truly were a younger sister who must bow to his greater knowledge and authority, and could be ordered about at will. Did he esteem her so little . . . or could it be that he was wary of esteeming her too much?

Chapter Five

When they returned to the house, it was quite late in the day, and they were both weary. Nick carried in the packages which had been stowed behind the carriage seat, and after mounting the stairs with the precious armload, he dumped it unceremoniously upon Amanda's bed. Announcing that he'd had quite enough of women for one day, he declared himself to be off in search of some decent food and company, and abruptly left her. Amanda paid little attention to this insult, however; she was only too grateful for the chance to be alone to sort out her thoughts, and perhaps even more importantly, to have a decent bath.

Discarding her new bonnet and cloak, she rang for a maid and requested a bath to be drawn, and a light supper tray which she could enjoy at leisure. At home, she had been accustomed to having to fend for herself, since the lone abigail's attention had been devoted mostly to Chloe. It was therefore a delicious treat to be looked after, and after Amanda had dismissed the servant and locked the door, she lowered herself into the bath with a blissful sigh.

The bath was refreshing to the body and soothing to the mind, but it brought no solutions to Amanda's dilemma. She had indeed escaped from the frightening fate wished upon her by her stepmother; but far from entering into a new life of independence, she was now more constrained than ever. She had to admit that her impulsive scheme of finding her friend had little chance of success, and without a sponsor to recommend her, it would be impossible to find genteel employment. And now, merely to save her abductor's good name, she was being pressured into accepting a new identity and perhaps even a forced marriage.

Of course, she could not truly be compelled to marry against her will, but the alternative was to leave Nick's protection and strike out on her own, with no employment and nowhere to live. Brave though she was, that prospect was daunting in the extreme.

There was only one other possibility, and that was the hope that a marriage might be arranged for her with someone whom she could love. When she tried to imagine such a man, however, it was Nick's face which lingered persistently in her mind, eluding all of her efforts to banish it. Finally she gave up the struggle, conceding to herself that until she could rid herself of this tiresome infatuation, marriage to any other man would be impossible to contemplate.

Sighing, Amanda dried herself off and slipped into the new nightdress which had been laid out for her. She then applied herself to the supper tray.

Once her meal was over and the tray had been removed, however, Amanda became aware of a restless boredom. At least Nick had a man's privilege of going about freely, enjoying the sights and sounds of Paris, but she was stuck here alone. Darkness had fallen long since, and she had to find some means of filling the long evening ahead. There were not even any books in her room, although perhaps the house possessed a library. With the servants retired to their own quarters, surely there would be no harm in slipping downstairs to investigate.

Fastening her robe tightly, Amanda took up a candle and made her way through the silent house, until she came upon the room she was seeking. The library was small and snug, and it was not long before she found a shelf of recent novels; either *Tante* Sophie had literary tastes or else she believed, like many ladies of society, that it was necessary to own the latest fashionable titles, even if one never even cracked open the first page. Amanda finally selected a novel by Monsieur Chateaubriand, and curled up in a large wing chair to read.

The candle was much lower in its socket, and Amanda was deeply engrossed in the adventures of the unfortunate René among the Indians in America, when the library door was suddenly thrown open, and the dark silhouette of a man appeared, aiming a pistol straight at Amanda's heart.

She uttered a stifled shriek and leaped to her feet, clutching the book in front of her as though it were a shield. First a highwayman, now a housebreaker—did she possess some fatal attraction for the criminal element? The man approached, and his angry expression faded into one of pure astonishment as he perceived her more closely. Indeed, the vision she presented was a startling one: a young woman with tumbled honey brown hair, clad in a ruffled pink nightrobe which, despite the fact that it covered her from chin to toe, did little to hide her slender curves. He examined her searchingly, from the tips of her slippers to her nervously-dilated eyes.

"Qui êtes-vous?" he demanded, striding toward her purposefully.

"Je suis—je m'appelle—" Amanda faltered, unnerved by his steady, menacing approach. Then as he reached out a hand to seize her arm, her knowledge of French deserted her completely. "Don't touch me!"

"Ah, you are English!" the man said in a heavily-accented voice, dropping his outstretched hand but keeping the weapon pointed at her. "Then please, you will tell me your name, and why you find yourself here in my house, yes?"

"In your—? Oh, you must be—oh, thank goodness! I thought—" Amanda collected herself with some difficulty. "I beg your pardon, my name is

Amanda Wa—'' She caught herself up just in time. "Malvern."

The man bowed slightly, still watching her with a perplexed wariness. "Malvern . . . You are related to Nicholas?" He pronounced the name in the French fashion, as "Nee-co-lah."

"Yes, I'm his sister." Amanda hoped that she sounded more convincing than she felt. "He brought me here last night. I'm sorry, I know it was dreadfully rude to arrive unannounced, but he seemed to think it would be all right."

He lowered the pistol abruptly and struck his forehead with one palm. "Ah, how I am a fool! Here I am, ready to shoot a thief, and she is a lovely lady who is the sister of my friend. Forgive me, mademoiselle." Much to Amanda's surprise, he bowed again, more deeply this time. "Allow me to present myself: I am Louis Auguste D'Aubreville, Comte de Richelet. I am delighted to welcome you, mademoiselle."

Amanda dropped a curtsey in reply, but as she did so, she was reminded of her unconventional attire. "I am very pleased to meet you, Monsieur le Comte," she said hurriedly. "With your permission, I will retire immediately. Nick is out, but when he returns, I'm certain that he can explain everything." She made as if to move past him, but he detained her with a light hand upon her arm.

"No, please, mademoiselle, stay a while. I would not wish to disturb you in your reading. It is I who will retire."

As he spoke, he led her back towards the light,

and Amanda received her first clear look at her host. He was a young man of medium height, with dark brown curly hair swept casually over a pale forehead; his eyes were also dark and intense beneath arched brows. He was undeniably good-looking, in a romantic style reminiscent of the notorious Lord Byron, but his attire showed nothing of that gentleman's disregard for fashion. On the contrary, he was dressed elegantly, even fastidiously.

With a swift engaging smile, he took her hand and imprinted a light kiss upon it; then he turned on his heel and left the room, closing the door quietly behind him. Unaccustomed to such gallantry, Amanda felt almost as flustered as the schoolgirl she was pretending to be; no matter how disreputable the Comte de Richelet's exploits might be, he certainly knew how to treat a lady—unlike some people! She stood for a moment lost in a reverie; and then she crept to the door, listening intently. As soon as everything was perfectly still, she slipped out of the library and fled back upstairs, locking her bedroom door securely. She reflected ruefully that it was becoming almost commonplace for people to be aiming pistols in her direction; upon that thought, a restless sleep finally claimed her.

When Amanda opened her eyes the next morning, she heard servants bustling about in the corridors, and knew that her meeting with the Comte de Richelet had not been merely a dream. Soon after, a young housemaid brought her a steaming cup of chocolate, and as Amanda sipped it gingerly, she recalled with some embarrassment the circumstances of last night's encounter. To counteract that unfortunate first impression, she dressed herself with particular care, combing her hair back from her forehead in the new style which, as well as flattering the shape of her face, made her look somewhat younger than her true age. It was regrettable that the gold-threaded muslin was still her only dress, but at least it was in the mode, and she hoped that other garments would arrive that afternoon. For the sake of appearances, Miss Amanda Malvern ought to have more than one dress to her name!

She descended the stairs and entered the breakfast parlor to find both Nick and the Comte already in attendance, with the remains of a large ham and several covered dishes bearing witness to their recent activities.

The Comte immediately rose to his feet, wishing her a good morning and inquiring after her rest. Amanda returned his warm smile as he brushed her fingertips with a light kiss. When she glanced at Nick, however, she was surprised to catch a scowl sharpening his features. She wondered briefly what had occurred to put him in an ill temper, but before she could speak, the Comte had followed her puzzled gaze, and was voicing her own thoughts. "Is something wrong, my friend, that you do not wish good morning to your sister?"

"Not at all," Nick snapped, wondering why

Louis hadn't let go of the blasted girl's hand. "I was merely thinking of something else. Good morning, Amanda; will you have coffee with us, or shall I ring for tea?"

"Coffee will do very well, thank you," she replied, seating herself in the empty chair next to him. It was odd, she reflected, as she listened to the conversation they resumed, how very different were the two men whom she could now observe at her leisure. Both were handsome, of course, but Nick was tall and lean, whereas the Comte was of ordinary height and build; and Nick was pale and fair in contrast to the Comte's dark good looks. Examining the Comte more closely, Amanda realized that there was almost no way to find fault with him: he was well groomed and dressed, handsome, and impeccably courteous. But somehow his regular features seemed bland next to Nick's angular handsomeness, and as she listened to their discussion, his wits seemed almost dull when pitted against Nick's razor-keen intelligence. Although to be quite fair, Amanda reminded herself, the Comte was speaking in English out of courtesy to his guests; perhaps he was more brilliant in his own tongue.

The object of her scrutiny turned suddenly and fastened his dark glowing eyes upon her. "Miss Malvern, since you have not seen anything of Paris, will you make me the honor to drive out with me today?"

Amanda smiled prettily at this rather convoluted speech. "Why, yes, thank you. That will be lovely—I've always wanted to see Paris." She cast a glance at Nick, and something in his face urged her to add, "That is, if my brother gives his permission."

"He would not be so cruel as to refuse," the Comte insisted. "After all, I am your cousin, and he knows that you would be quite safe with me." Nick made a rather derisive sound which the Comte ignored. "If he prefers, my groom will ride behind us, *en chaperon*."

"Oh, very well, Louis," Nick acquiesced. "I've got to rig myself out in some decent clothes today, so you may as well take the chit to see the town. Just take care not to let her out of your sight." So saying, he looked straitly at Amanda, and the warning in those pale green eyes was unmistakable.

The Comte laughed, his dark eyes smiling at Amanda. "I assure you, my friend, that is the last thing I would wish to happen." He reached out to pat her hand in a paternal fashion, though the feather-light caress of his fingertips was not paternal at all; after a polite hesitation, Amanda drew her hand gently away, glancing at Nick to see if he had noticed the brief exchange. There was no indication that he had, however, and she unconsciously relaxed.

"Before we leave, mademoiselle, I must present you to *Maman*. She arrived last night, and will be most ravished to make your acquaintance."

Here was a moment of truth indeed: if Nick's aunt did not accept her, the whole plan was in jeopardy. Casting a panicked glance in Nick's direction, and receiving only an amused nod in response, Amanda followed Louis upstairs in some trepidation. She was ushered into a large, opulently furnished bedchamber. Without ceremony, Louis approached the bed, upon which lay a lady whose dark coloring resembled his, but who was of indeterminate age and considerable girth. Her heavy-lidded eyes watched their advent without evident curiosity, as she took delicate sips at a Sèvres teacup.

"Maman," he said in rapid French. "This is Mademoiselle Amanda Malvern. She is the sister of Nicholas, who has come to make us a visit for a few weeks." Then he turned to Amanda, addressing her in English. "Mademoiselle, allow me to present my mother, the Comtesse de Richelet."

Amanda dropped an automatic curtsey, as she was subjected to a slow but unnervingly-thorough scrutiny. At last, when the silence seemed to stretch to screaming point, the lady spoke aloud.

"So you are Amanda," she drawled, in a languid, softly accented voice. "Come here, *ma petite*, and you may kiss me." Amanda did as she was bid. "I hope that you will enjoy your visit; I find it much too fatiguing to go out and about much myself, but my son will take good care of you. And your charming brother, of course. Louis, send Nicholas up to me please. Au revoir, *ma petite*." And with these few words of dismissal, she waved Amanda out of her presence.

As soon as she was out in the corridor, it was

impossible to hold back a small sigh of relief. *Tante* Sophie was autocratic in her own way, but she was far too self-centered and indolent to observe her young guest too closely, or to ask awkward questions. On the other hand, of course, her disinterest closed off the possibility that Amanda might ask her for assistance in finding Celia, or if worse came to worst, in seeking some form of genteel employment. Amanda was still on her own as much as ever before.

Only a short time later, Amanda was more than happy to be escorted out into the sunshine and handed gently into the same phaeton which she had driven the day before. It was a fine day, and once more it was impossible not to be optimistic. This was Paris, after all! The Comte made a great show of handling the ribbons, although he was no more than a competent whip, and Amanda had to hide a smile, thinking that if she had truly been a schoolgirl, she would have been most impressed by the Comte's display.

Honesty prevented her from complimenting the Comte upon his driving, and so she made a particular effort to encourage his conversation. This proved to be easy, for despite his fractured English, Louis was an accomplished escort, and she found herself charmingly entertained. He was also quite willing to satisfy her curiosity about the city's history, and obligingly drove her through the Marais, a once-elegant quarter which had housed the wealthiest of sixteenth- and seventeenth-century aristocracy. Most of the grand houses had been sadly neglected, or even vandalized during the War, but there was still evidence of its former grandeur, and the elegant stone arches and brick façades of the Place des Vosges made Amanda sigh in genuine admiration.

The small sound brought the Comte's attention to her glowing face, and his eyes gleamed with appreciation and perhaps the merest hint of speculation, before his face resumed its expression of bland amusement.

There was a small park in the center of the Place, with shade trees and benches, and the Comte invited Amanda to take a stroll at his side. She allowed him to hand her down from the phaeton, and they began a leisurely walk. The Comte lost no time in engaging Amanda in an avid flirtation, designed to turn the head of any unfledged miss. Amanda was in no such danger, but it was nonetheless a new and heady sensation, for her social experience in the past had been limited to those painful weeks in London. There, she had never been truly at her ease, at first suffering Peter's absence, and then mourning his death. Her natural high spirits had carried her through the experience, and she had had several admirers, but she had never received attention from the pinks of the *ton*.

This situation, however, was entirely different. Now she was dressed in the height of fashion, and being assiduously courted by a man who might have embodied a young woman's romantic ideal. What was more, Amanda now had the poise and maturity to enjoy a situation which in the past would have thrown her into confusion. The only difficulty was not to reveal her true age, and though summoning a blush was rather beyond her, Amanda managed a few winsome smiles before embarking upon a campaign to divert the Comte's attention to other matters.

Encouraged by Amanda's skillful questioning and admiring glances, the Comte was only too happy to talk about himself for a good twenty minutes. After a time, however, he began to inquire about her own background, and despite her best efforts he refused to be sidetracked.

"Tell me, Miss Malvern," he coaxed, "I must know more of your relation to my friend Nicholas. He said that you are his sister, but not ever have I heard him speak of you before."

"I am only his half sister," Amanda stated, repeating Nick's spur-of-the-moment invention. "We have never lived in the same household. In fact, we had scarcely ever seen each other before this trip."

"Indeed?" the Comte replied. "But then why did your family send you to rest with him?"

She thought rapidly. "I'm afraid I have almost no family other than Nicky. I was living with an elderly cousin, but she has recently become ill, and could not sponsor me in society."

"Aha," the Comte nodded wisely. "That would explain why you had no female relative as an accompaniment. And there were no family friends or neighbors?"

"No—we lived in the countryside, quite remote from anyone else, and the family did not socialize." The fiction was becoming more and more complicated, and Amanda began to feel nervous of making a slip. She could only hope that the Comte would regard her strange story as evidence of typical English eccentricity! "I would have had my abigail," she added, "but the wretched girl became ill on the boat, and we had to leave her in Calais. Nicky has promised to hire me someone as soon as possible."

"Allow me, mademoiselle," the Comte bowed slightly. "I shall direct one of my mother's own maids to serve you."

"Thank you, Monsieur le Comte," Amanda replied with a sinking heart, neatly trapped by her own words. She could only hope that the maid would not gossip above or belowstairs about her lack of baggage.

"Please, Miss Malvern—you will call me Louis? I do not wish to be formal with you, as you are the sister of my dear friend and cousin—and therefore, you are my own cousin as well."

"Very well, then, Louis, and you shall call me Amanda." She was rewarded by a dazzling smile revealing his even white teeth.

"You make me very happy, Amanda," he murmured softly, squeezing her hand as it rested upon his arm. "I have a great desire to know you better . . . much better."

Amanda stopped in her tracks, assailed by an uncomfortable realization. She had not anticipated having to fend off unwanted suitors quite so soon! It appeared nonetheless that Louis's intentions went beyond a mere flirtation, and it was imperative that she put an end to any hopes he might be cherishing.

"Louis, I wish to be your friend," she said seriously, "but I cannot be anything more to you."

He was somewhat startled by this unexpected frankness. "Why not?"

Amanda opened her mouth and then shut it abruptly. How could she tell him that she was not who she appeared to be, but only a penniless adventuress? Strangely enough, however, that very thought brought inspiration. She leaned closer to him, whispering conspiratorially. "I must tell you a very great secret, which you must promise never to mention to anyone else, not even your mother. Do you so promise?"

"Yes, of course," Louis replied, much puzzled.

She drew a deep breath and commenced her tale. "Our father was a very great eccentric, who believed that women should be independent, and earn their own living in the world. When he died, he left all of the estate to Nick, and nothing to me. And the worst of it is," she dropped her voice to a tragic whisper, "it is stipulated that Nick cannot give me a dowry!"

"But that is a cruelty! A barbarity!"

"Yes, indeed," she agreed mournfully. "But there is nothing which can be done. Nicky has always provided for my needs, but if he attempts to settle any money upon me, he will lose his whole fortune."

Louis looked decidedly crestfallen, but whether

from sympathy for her or from disappointment at the frustration of his own schemes, Amanda could not tell. She rather suspected the latter cause, especially as his clasp upon her hand had become very faint. However, she took pity upon his confusion.

"I told you this because you are a friend, and it would be unfair to deceive you about my circumstances. Not that I believe for one minute that it would make any difference to you! But I am aware of what you owe your noble name and family honor. You must marry someone of equal birth and fortune."

"How understanding you are, Amanda!" Louis breathed, obviously much relieved at this opportunity to save face.

"Of course, I understand," she consoled. "No matter what your personal wishes may be, you have your duty to fulfill. And now, the second reason I have told you this, is that I know that I can trust you not to reveal what I have said to anyone else. You realize that it would be fatal to all my hopes!"

"Yes, I do," Louis nodded. "But you must not worry, Amanda. I know that you will have a great success in Paris, so lovely and charming as you are. And assure yourself, your trust in me shall not be deplaced."

Amanda looked blank for a second, and then smiled. "I believe you mean 'misplaced.' Thank you, dear Louis, but I'm afraid that I know very little of how to go on in French society." And that, she admitted with regret, was absolutely true, although not because of her presumed youth. "Perhaps we might make an arrangement: if you would help me with my French, and teach me how to behave properly, I could help you with your English!"

"An excellent idea!" Louis smiled. "I shall be very much content to be your teacher, although you need no lessons in how to be charming. You will captivate everyone." For once, he spoke entirely without guile.

Amanda shook her head laughingly. "Very well, here is your first question: how does one respond to ridiculous extravagant compliments?"

They continued their stroll in excellent humor. Once the understanding between them had been reached, Amanda was pleased to find that Louis dropped his courtly manner, and began to treat her with a certain fatherly indulgence, as if she were indeed a precocious schoolgirl. In turn, she relaxed in his company and found herself addressing him in the bantering terms she had once used with Peter.

Their harmonious rapport was also due in part to the fact that Louis's vanity was flattered by her appeal to his greater social expertise. He was clever enough to know that her success under his wing would enhance his own status, and furthermore, he felt truly grateful for Amanda's frankness, which had prevented him from pursuing what would have been a very ill-chosen and ultimately embarrassing courtship.

Upon their return to the house, they found Nick mysteriously absent. *Tante* Sophie was accustomed to take luncheon in her room, and so after Louis and Amanda partook of their own refreshment, they resolved to go into the parlor and begin her social instruction immediately. They commenced with forms of address and greeting, and though no fault could be found with Amanda's graceful curtsey, there was so much more that these Frenchmen considered important: how deep to sink, when to nod, how many fingers to extend, where to focus the eyes. As Louis assured her, these signs were vital, marking the differences between old and young, high rank and low, husbands and lovers.

Amanda took Louis's directives as a kind of challenge. She was well aware that a life of high society was not to be her ultimate fate, but the temptation was nonetheless very great to make a brief splash while she could. In addition, it would be intensely gratifying to show certain persons (unnamed, of course) that she could indeed be found attractive.

The lengthening shadows went unnoticed as the two applied themselves to Amanda's lessons, and neither of them heard Nick walk into the room, just returned from a long day spent with his tailor.

Amanda was perched upon the settee, waving a delicate fan in one hand while the other was clasped tightly by Louis, seated next to her. He raised it to his lips, and spoke in French, his tone urgent.

"Come with me to the garden. I must see you alone."

In response, Amanda held her open fan over her heart. "Indeed, Monsieur, it is very warm in here," she answered in French, making subtle play with her long lashes.

As he watched, Nick felt a surge of irritation which he could not quite explain. So, the minx had lost no time in his absence, and was casting lures in Louis's direction. He leaned back against the shadowed wall, crossing his arms and glowering as he watched to see what would happen next.

To his surprise, Louis stood up and clapped his hands in delight. "Excellent! That was *formidable!*"

"You mean wonderful," Amanda smiled up at him.

"Yes, yes. Now, again, and this time, you shall be offended." He seated himself and took hold of her hand once more. "Come with me to the garden," he repeated.

Amanda stiffened her posture and raised her chin to look at him squarely. She snapped her fan shut and laid it across his wrist. "People are watching, Monsieur," she said coldly.

Nick could no longer contain himself. "What the devil is going on here?" he barked, striding into the center of the room.

Amanda and Louis both jumped to their feet, startled. They were still holding hands, like two children, and Amanda felt a traitorous flush stealing over her cheeks. It was caused, however, not by a sense of guilt, but by the simple shock of seeing Nick again.

Louis was the first one to find his tongue. "How you startled us, my friend! I have been teaching your sister a few rules of etiquette."

"And what else have you been teaching her? Or she teaching you?" Nick asked sardonically.

"Oh, yes, she is helping me with my barbarous English," Louis replied, missing the insulting thrust of Nick's remark. Amanda, however, was fully aware of Nick's implication, and hastily dropped Louis's hand.

"Louis has been extremely kind," she asserted with a hint of defiance. "You see, I have explained to him the painful nature of our family circumstances."

"Our—?"

"Alas, yes," she interrupted hastily. "Every unfortunate detail. And Louis has agreed to keep our secret."

"You need not fear, my friend," Louis interposed, moving to rest a comforting hand upon Nick's shoulder. "I have nothing but admiration for you and for your brave little sister."

"Will you excuse us for a moment?" Nick seized Amanda's arm and began to propel her out of the room, as Louis nodded in puzzled agreement.

As soon as the door closed behind them, Nick stopped and glared down at her. "Just what are our 'painful family circumstances'?"

"Shhh! Not here! Come with me to the garden," Amanda hissed, unconsciously echoing Louis's earlier phrase.

It did not escape Nick's notice, however. "Should

I be flattered? I recall that you refused Louis that honor."

"Don't be ridiculous!" she snapped. "That was merely playacting."

"Was it? Then I congratulate you; I found it most convincing."

They had arrived in the garden, and Amanda turned impatiently to face him. "Do try not to be unpleasant for just one moment, and listen to me. I had to tell him that I was penniless."

"I thought I told you to say nothing," Nick said irritably. "Did you forget so soon, or were his soulful looks so persuasive?"

"Neither one, for heaven's sake! But I couldn't allow him to propose to me, thinking that I was a rich heiress."

"Are you sure that was the type of proposal he had in mind?"

Amanda's hand itched to slap his face. He saw her slight movement, and captured her wrist with a deceptively light hold. "Don't do that, my girl," he murmured. "Don't even think it. Louis may be watching us from inside."

"You and your insinuations are utterly insufferable!" Amanda asserted roundly. "But I wouldn't demean myself by striking you. It's quite safe to let me go."

Nick released her, somewhat warily. "Very well, then, for purposes of this discussion, we shall assume that Louis did indeed begin to court you. Now, what in the world did you tell him about the family?"

She could not help smiling with grim enjoyment. "I told him that Father was a great eccentric who believed in women's independence from men. I said that the estate was entailed so that you could not settle a dowry upon me—and that if you *tried*, you would lose the entirety of your fortune!"

Nick stared at her as if she had suddenly lost her reason. Then the corners of his mouth began to twitch into an unwilling smile. "Surely he did not believe such a faradiddle as that!" he scoffed.

"On the contrary, he was entirely convinced," Amanda protested, stifling a giggle. "Indeed, he found the story quite pathetic. If I may say so, I thought it rather touching myself. And besides, Nick, you were going to have to invent some such tale sooner or later. I merely saved you the trouble."

"I am eternally in your debt," Nick replied sarcastically. "But I wonder, why did you not allow him to declare himself? Mind you, I like him too well to have allowed him to fall into any trap of our making, but there was nothing to stop you from trying."

Amanda sighed. Once again, it seemed, she and Nick had established a brief rapport, only to have it slip away. And as before, it was Nick's determination to think the worst of her which caused the breach. "Your opinion of me is refreshingly consistent," Amanda declared ironically. "Think what you please, but he is your friend, and he is being very kind to us both. I would not serve him such an ill turn."

His pale eyes scanned her face intently. "You are certainly full of surprises, Amanda. I can't help wondering what schemes are hatching behind that innocent face of yours."

"You'd have no difficulty at all, if you'd realize that not everyone acts according to your own selfish rules," she retorted.

An angry gleam sharpened his regard. "Ah, yes, and I'd forgotten what an adder's tongue you've got. Well, selfish I may be, Amanda, but I don't care to have my behavior examined by such as you." And with those contemptuous words, he firmly escorted her back into the house, unaware that she was grateful for the pressure of his hand upon her elbow, because for some strange reason, her vision was slightly blurred.

Chapter Six

That very evening, as they met in the small salon before dinner, Louis announced that he had received a card of invitation to an informal *soirée* at the home of Madame Demorest.

"She must have heard that you are here, Nicholas, because she includes you and Amanda in her invitation. What do you think? Shall we go?"

Nick nodded thoughtfully. "It will do for a start. Liliane could do much to launch Amanda into society, if she chose."

Louis laughed. "Me, I think that one would do anything *you* chose."

The two men exchanged a knowing smile, while Amanda bristled in her seat. Perhaps Louis considered her too naïve to comprehend his innuendo, but for Nick there was absolutely no excuse to flaunt his amours in such a manner. She cast him a smouldering glance which, upon its interception, earned her one of Nick's most ironically amused stares.

"It is well arranged, then, for tomorrow night," Louis continued, unaware of that brief exchange. "Amanda has been such a quick student, that I think she will do excellently. But for another thing—does she know how to dance?"

"Yes, I do," Amanda interposed, irritated at being discussed as though she were not present. "But I'm afraid what I learned in the country must be shockingly old-fashioned." If only he knew, she grimaced inwardly, that her skills were five whole years out of date!

"Then later I shall show you," Louis declared, and indeed, immediately after the meal he embarked upon a new set of lessons with renewed enthusiasm. An hour, and then two, passed with speed and a good deal of laughter, as Amanda's rusty skills were gradually honed. Despite her enjoyment, however, she found herself wondering why it was that dancing with Louis failed to arouse the slightest flutter in her breast. After all, he was handsome, graceful, and quite complimentary about her dancing abilities. But the warm clasp of his hands was singularly unexciting, and as he smiled into her eyes, she was aware only of the fact that he was nearly the same height as she. Perhaps if he had been taller . . . much taller . . .

After a late sleep the following morning, Amanda's lessons continued on throughout the day. Nick was absent during this time, evincing little interest in the proceedings, although Amanda reflected bitterly that he would notice quickly enough if she were to embarrass him in any way. Louis, however, was so quick to offer encourage-

MORE PASSION AND ADVENTURE AWAIT... YOUR TRIP TO A BIG ADVENTUROUS WORLD BEGINS WHEN YOU ACCEPT YOUR FIRST 4 NOVELS ABSOLUTELY *FREE* (AN $18.00 VALUE)

Accept your Free gift and start to experience more of the passion and adventure you like in a historical romance novel. Each Zebra novel is filled with proud men, spirited women and tempestuous love that you'll remember long after you turn the last page.

Zebra Historical Romances are the finest novels of their kind. They are written by authors who really know how to weave tales of romance and adventure in the historical settings you love. You'll feel like you've actually gone back in time with the thrilling stories that each Zebra novel offers.

GET YOUR FREE GIFT WITH THE START OF YOUR HOME SUBSCRIPTION

Our readers tell us that these books sell out very fast in book stores and often they miss the newest titles. So Zebra has made arrangements for you to receive the four newest novels published each month.

You'll be guaranteed that you'll never miss a title, and home delivery is so convenient. And to show you just how easy it is to get Zebra Historical Romances, we'll send you your first 4 books absolutely FREE! Our gift to you just for trying our home subscription service.

BIG SAVINGS AND FREE HOME DELIVERY

Each month, you'll receive the four newest titles as soon as they are published. You'll probably receive them even before the bookstores do. What's more, you may preview these exciting novels free for 10 days. If you like them as much as we think you will, just pay the low preferred subscriber's price of just $3.75 each. *You'll save $3.00 each month off the publisher's price.* AND, your savings are even greater because there are never any shipping, handling or other hidden charges—FREE Home Delivery. Of course you can return any shipment within 10 days for full credit, no questions asked. There is no minimum number of books you must buy.

4 FREE BOOKS

TO GET YOUR 4 FREE BOOKS WORTH $18.00 — MAIL IN THE FREE BOOK CERTIFICATE T O D A Y

Fill in the Free Book Certificate below, and we'll send your FREE BOOKS to you as soon as we receive it.

If the certificate is missing below, write to: Zebra Home Subscription Service, Inc., P.O. Box 5214, 120 Brighton Road, Clifton, New Jersey 07015-5214.

FREE BOOK CERTIFICATE
4 FREE BOOKS

ZEBRA HOME SUBSCRIPTION SERVICE, INC.

YES! Please start my subscription to Zebra Historical Romances and send me my first 4 books absolutely FREE. I understand that each month I may preview four new Zebra Historical Romances free for 10 days. If I'm not satisfied with them, I may return the four books within 10 days and owe nothing. Otherwise, I will pay the low preferred subscriber's price of just $3.75 each; a total of $15.00, *a savings off the publisher's price of $3.00.* I may return any shipment and I may cancel this subscription at any time. There is no obligation to buy any shipment and there are no shipping, handling or other hidden charges. Regardless of what I decide, the four free books are mine to keep.

NAME

ADDRESS   APT

CITY   STATE   ZIP

(   )
TELEPHONE

SIGNATURE   (If under 18, parent or guardian must sign)

Terms, offer and prices subject to change without notice. Subscription subject to acceptance by Zebra Books. Zebra Books reserves the right to reject any order or cancel any subscription.

GET
FOUR
FREE
BOOKS
(AN $18.00 VALUE)

ZEBRA HOME SUBSCRIPTION
SERVICE, INC.
P.O. Box 5214
120 BRIGHTON ROAD
CLIFTON, NEW JERSEY, 07015-5214

ment, that when the hour finally came for her to dress for the evening, she was almost ready to believe his promises for her imminent success.

Her new maid Martine informed her shyly that several new dresses had been delivered that afternoon, and Amanda wasted a great deal of time trying to decide what might be suitable. She eventually chose a dress of pale green lawn, whose simple, classical lines flattered her slender figure and made her skin seem very white. Gazing at her reflection in the mirror, Amanda knew instinctively that she would have looked better in a deeper shade of green, and a bodice which revealed more of her graceful neck and shoulders; unfortunately, such things were forbidden to unmarried young girls. Remembering Madame Demorest's flamboyant appearance, she felt a moment's chagrin at the masquerade which forced her to conceal her true age and identity.

Then she gave herself a mental shake. True, she was not glamorous and alluring, and her social experience was woefully limited. But she was still Amanda Waverley, the girl who had never shied from a high fence. She would show them all that she was not to be intimidated, and that by birth at least she was their equal. So, holding herself regally erect, she went to join the gentlemen downstairs.

As she descended the steps, she saw Nick waiting in the foyer, and as he turned around, she paused and drew an involuntary breath. He was dressed in a smooth-fitting coat of midnight blue, with pale gray pantaloons which molded his muscular thighs without a wrinkle. The neck-points of his shirt were crisply starched, and around his neck was a gray silk cravat tied in an intricate design and fastened with a gleaming sapphire stickpin. Gone was his habitual air of tousled negligence; Nick was now a veritable model of elegant fashion.

"Well, what are you staring at?" he asked with a slight frown.

"You!" Amanda confessed. She descended the steps quite slowly, still regarding him with a startled air.

"Why? What's wrong with me?" he pursued in faint consternation.

"Nothing! It's just that you—you're so—"

"What?!"

"Beautiful." The word escaped her before she could stop herself, and she flushed in embarrassment. What a foolish thing to say to a man!

A little smile tugged at the corners of his mouth. "I believe that is supposed to be my line. As it happens, you look rather well yourself. Come here."

Amanda took a hesitant step closer, so that she had to tilt her head back to look up into his face. Nick removed a small box from his waistcoat pocket and handed it to her. "Here," he said, "this is something I picked up this afternoon."

She opened the box, and found a small but perfect string of pearls lying against the soft velvet. "Oh, Nick," she exclaimed, "they're lovely!"

"I saw them, and knew they'd be just the thing for a young girl's debut. I'd never live it down if my sister were seen without a single gewgaw."

Amanda's soaring heart landed with a thud. So he had not bought them as a gift, a token of friendship, but to save his own pride. It was a lucky thing that he had spoken so quickly, for she had been about to throw her arms around his neck to thank him.

"It is very kind of you," she managed to say in a cool formal tone. "Of course, I shall return them when we part company."

"If you like," he replied casually. "Perhaps if you're cooperative, I'll let you keep them as a wedding present."

Amanda could not respond to this, as her throat felt suddenly tight. Drat the man, did he always have to harp upon unpleasant matters? She turned her back upon him and moved towards the mirror in the hall, fumbling with the clasp of the pearls. Before she knew it, however, she felt his strong fingers close over hers.

"You'll never do it that way. Let go." His voice was impatient; as he fastened the clasp for her, however, his fingers lingered unnecessarily, stroking her skin with a light, caressing touch. "You've got a pretty neck, Amanda," he said, almost unwillingly, and as her heart seemed to miss a beat, he bent to press a kiss upon her delicate nape. "It's a pity I'm always wanting to wring it."

At that moment—mercifully for Amanda's composure—Louis appeared in the doorway, announcing that the carriage was ready. He also was attired in elegant evening dress, which perfectly complemented his dark handsomeness. Though Nick towered over him in height, Louis was well-proportioned and, as always, complete to a shade. Amanda allowed him to fasten her cloak for her, and took his arm, unable for the life of her to look at Nick.

By the time they arrived at Madame Demorest's, Amanda had recovered her self-assurance, determined that she would not allow Nick's perplexing manner to distract her from the unaccustomed pleasure of a social evening. As they stepped into the wide foyer, however, Amanda's spirits suffered yet another setback. Instead of the quiet intimate gathering she had been led to expect, there were at least seventy persons in the salon ahead. The room glittered with candles and with women's jewels, and Amanda realized with a sinking feeling that she was going to be woefully out of place in that sophisticated throng.

Involuntarily she clutched Louis's arm, but he merely laughed as he patted her hand. "I should have warned you, Amanda; Liliane's notion of informal is something quite out of the ordinary. But don't worry—your brother and I will take care of you. Here comes Liliane now!"

Their hostess swept up with a rustle of silken skirts and a cloud of expensive perfume. She was dressed in brilliant green, her favorite color, with diamonds dangling from her ears and circling her throat and wrists. Her dark hair was piled into stylish curls, with several locks artfully loosened to sweep against her creamy white neck.

"How delightful to see you!" Liliane breathed in French, directing her gaze first at Nick and then Louis. She leaned over slightly as she extended her hand, exposing a generous amount of cleavage; both men kissed the proffered fingertips as expected, but it seemed to a vexed Amanda that they lingered over the business a good deal longer than was necessary. Liliane's red lips were parted in a suggestive smile which Amanda found almost as distasteful as the answering gleam in Nick's pale eyes.

"I see you have brought the little girl, as well." Liliane's voice dripped with condescension, and Amanda reacted instinctively. She met the woman's scornful gaze with a slightly awed smile and dipped a slight curtsey. "I am so honored to be here with your older friends, Madame," she said. "Indeed, when I see you, I feel very, very young!"

Liliane's eyes glittered for a moment, but Amanda's face reflected only innocent candor. Louis struggled to hide a smile, while Nick threw a narrowed glance in Amanda's direction. Immediately she sensed the danger of overplaying her hand, and took steps to recover Liliane's good will with flattery. "How I wish," Amanda continued quite truthfully, "that I could wear such a ravishingly beautiful gown!"

The simple stratagem was effective, as Liliane preened visibly. "You are sweet to say so, Miss Malvern," she gushed. "What a shame that young girls must always wear such insipid colors."

Amanda raised her chin an inch, still smiling serenely although the insult rankled. Upon the two men watching, however, Liliane's spiteful comment had quite a different effect. Amanda looked far from insipid; in fact, compared to

117

Liliane's flamboyance, Amanda possessed a delicate grace. Next to bright emerald and rows of diamonds, her pale green dress and pearls had the elegance and freshness of a water lily.

Glancing up at the men's expressions, Liliane suddenly realized her error, and hastened to retrieve her position. "Come with me, Nicholas," she urged, taking possessive hold of his arm. "There are so many people for you to meet! You will excuse us," she called over her shoulder, as she pulled Nick into the crowded room. Louis and Amanda were left to follow behind.

They were not alone for long, however. Louis took it upon himself to perform the duties of a host, and Amanda was soon surrounded by new acquaintances. He drew her from one group to the next, pleased to see that she remembered her brief lessons as she smiled and curtsied.

Soon the room was abuzz over the mysterious newcomer who carried herself so regally, yet had such a lovely warm smile. As a protégée of the Comte de Richelet, she was received politely by all; but it was her attractiveness and charm that kept people talking of her after she had moved on.

The evening had been well along when they had arrived, and so it was a scant half-hour later that the musicians struck up the first notes. Amanda was slightly bewildered to find herself at the center of a crush of men seeking her hand for the first dance. The matter was easily settled, as Louis was still by her side; smiling prettily at the others, she announced that the first dance was already promised. Louis was quick to respond to her meaningful pinch, and so the two of them moved onto the dance floor.

"Thank you, Louis," she said gratefully. "I simply could not face dancing with a stranger. What if I made a wrong step?"

"No need to worry," Louis reassured her, guiding her with a light touch. "You dance quite delightfully. In fact, you are making me very proud tonight."

Amanda felt a glow of pleasure at the compliment, as she saw that Louis's dark eyes were warm with sincerity. They exchanged a quick smile, which did not go unnoticed by their onlookers.

"So, our Louis is captivated by a mere schoolgirl," Liliane whispered spitefully into Nick's ear. "I suppose your little sister is well dowered?"

Nick's mouth tightened into a hard line as he watched the dancers. Then he shrugged his broad shoulders. "Louis has a kind heart," he answered evasively, turning aside her question. "Do you care for more champagne?"

Amanda was oblivious of being watched as Louis was succeeded by a series of new partners. She was lost in the enjoyment of the moment, and to the jaded socialites present, her enthusiasm was refreshing. She had never received so much flattering attention before, and while she did not believe for one moment that she was truly as beautiful as she was being told, still the pretense was exciting.

Before long, Amanda began to weary, and she felt obliged to give her next admirer a polite refusal. He was so crestfallen, however, that she rapidly amended her words, asking instead for his company while she enjoyed a brief rest. The young man brightened immediately, and the two sat down upon a sofa in a nearby alcove.

He had been introduced to her earlier as Philippe de Colombe, and he was a rather ordinary-looking young man of about nineteen, dressed in a style which struck Amanda as being a bit extreme. His shirt points were a shade too high, and his shoulders were padded a shade too thickly, as if his tailor were compensating for the immaturity of his physique. But his eyes were a warm brown, exuding such sincere friendliness that Amanda found herself softening in response.

Philippe's youth made him marvelously easy to talk to, and Amanda enjoyed quizzing him about his school experiences and his recent travels into Italy. It became clear that he was a very wealthy, but very lonely young man who had spent his life surrounded by tutors. Only now was he beginning to spread his wings, and hostesses like Liliane Demorest found him amusingly anxious to please. Of course, he was aware of none of this; but Amanda was quick to perceive his underlying lack of confidence, and so she made a special effort to draw him out. Within a very few minutes, they were chatting with the familiarity of old friends.

From across the room, Nick watched the two of them with an impassive expression. Liliane had disappeared for the moment, and he felt disinclined to pursue any of the other women whose glances had beckoned him. Instead, his eyes returned to Amanda again and again.

Apparently she had found herself a willing

young pup, but the fact that she seemed to be obeying his instructions brought him no pleasure. It only seemed to confirm that she was every bit as calculating as the rest of her sex, just as he had suspected. Even so, he told himself, it would be wise to have a private word with her, to make certain everything was going according to plan.

He strolled over to the alcove and gave Amanda a slight bow. "I don't wish to interrupt, my dear," he drawled, "but I thought perhaps you might have saved a dance for me."

Amanda was startled, but recovered quickly. "Why, yes, of course!" She glanced at Philippe's uncertain expression, as he beheld this tall virile stranger who evidently held a prior claim. "Monsieur, I would like you to meet my brother, Sir Nicholas Malvern. Nicky, this is Monsieur Philippe de Colombe."

Philippe rose to his feet with obvious relief etched upon his young face, and the two men shook hands. Nick accorded him a brief nod, and then pulled Amanda into his arms as the music struck up for the next dance.

For the first few moments, neither of them spoke as they moved together to the strains of soft music. Amanda strove to concentrate upon the steps, fighting the distraction of Nick's nearness. It was virtually hopeless, however, with the feel of his strong hand enclosing hers, and the sheer size of him, which forced her to look upwards to meet his gaze. And in his turn, Nick was acutely aware of the delicacy of her hand in his, and the warmth of her body beneath the thin fabric where his other hand rested lightly. They executed several more turns before Nick recollected what he had come to say.

Before he could speak, however, Amanda herself was prompted to break the spell between them. "Did you decide to do the gentlemanly thing by standing up with your sister, or were you wishing to critique my dancing?" she teased.

"Neither one," he replied absently. "Although since you mention it, you ought to be bending your knee more on the demiturns. Otherwise, however, your steps are quite passable for a beginner."

Amanda's eyes sparkled with indignation. "You are too kind, I'm sure. I shall do my best not to tread upon your toes. But may I ask why *did* you stand up with me, if not for the pleasure of my company?"

Nick glanced down at the evident temper in her upturned face. "Smile, my dear," he reproved softly. "We mustn't give the impression of quarrelling. What I meant to say—" They were separated briefly by the movement of the dance, but then he caught her to him once more. "What I meant to say was that I'm pleased you've agreed to cooperate, and I approve your choice."

"My choice?" she asked in bewilderment. "What choice?"

He cast a quizzical look in her direction. "I mean your choice of suitors, of course. They tell me young De Colombe is one of the richest young men in the city. But I imagine you knew that already."

"I did not!" Amanda protested. "And he's scarcely a suitor after only one dance."

"You're forgetting to smile," Nick remonstrated. "As I was saying, I approve your choice. He's young, rich, and no doubt as foolish as most boys of that age. But you'll have to be wary of the competition; there will be girls who are wealthier and more attractive dangling after such a prize."

Amanda obliged him with a smile that was more akin to a grimace, and he quirked an eyebrow in mock surprise.

"Oh, have I wounded your sensibilities?" he drawled. "Were you perhaps expecting me to praise your incomparable loveliness, which outshines every other woman in the room?"

She flashed him a look which might have impaled him to the wall. "Not at all. I am vastly relieved to hear the unflattering truth. As a matter of fact, I am quite fatigued by other men's endless compliments, and I find your boorishness rather refreshing."

Nick's eyes glowed green with amusement, and for once his smile was genuine. "*Touché!* Very well, I shall be quite unoriginal, and tell you that your eyes sparkle delightfully when you are angry. I do believe . . ." He knit his brows as though pondering an important plea. "Yes, there's no doubt about it. With those eyes, the proper stone for you is yellow topaz. Make sure you tell your little Philippe."

Amanda stiffened in his grasp. "He is not 'my little Philippe,' and you are a beast!" she hissed softly. Nick's smile deepened slightly, and he made no reply, merely tightening his grasp as the musicians struck up for another dance. Unfortunately for Amanda's peace of mind, it was a waltz.

While the dance was still frowned upon in England, especially for young girls, the freer society of Paris had accepted it some time since. But Amanda could understand why it was considered dangerous, as she whirled around the room in Nick's arms. His hand pressed into the small of her back, pulling her against his chest as the swirling motion of the waltz nearly lifted her feet from the ground. With her left hand clutching his broad shoulder for support, her right hand was clasped tightly in his strong grip. Amanda's heart began to pound wildly in her breast, as she felt his body pressed intimately against her. Suddenly everything was forgotten, except the nearness of this man, and her own involuntary response . . . and then abruptly the dance was over. Nick brought them to a smooth halt, and held her tightly for a brief instant; their eyes locked, and Amanda saw his eyes burning with an intense, though inscrutable emotion. Then he released her, making a small sardonic bow before turning away into the crowd.

Slightly dazed, Amanda made her way through the throng of people and stepped out into the garden. The air was cool and refreshing, and she found a bench where she would be hidden from view. As she sank down upon it gratefully, her senses were still caught up in that dizzying waltz. It had taken her by surprise, and she could not help

124

fearing that she might have revealed too much of her feelings for him in that final, unguarded moment. Nick was too perceptive by far, and if he should ever suspect the depth of her attraction to him . . . And what of his own reaction? He had been affected as well, but he guarded his feelings too closely for her to guess the truth. She could only hope that it was not contempt for herself which she had read in those blazing green eyes.

After ten minutes, her heartbeat had slowed to normal, and her skin no longer felt hot to the touch. As she was about to rise and return to the salon, however, she heard voices approach, stopping within a few feet of where she was concealed.

"Oh, *mon cher*, how I have waited for this!" It was Liliane Demorest. "You say tonight?"

"Yes. Tonight." The blood seemed to freeze in Amanda's veins, as she recognized Nick's voice, low and caressing.

"But what about your sister? Will she not suspect something?"

"No, why should she? I'll send her home with Louis, and she'll go straight to bed; then tomorrow, I'll simply say that I arrived late, and did not wish to wake her. She's a gullible creature."

Amanda felt the nails digging into her clenched palms. Less than five minutes ago, he had held her in his arms, and now here he was, arranging an assignation with that odious woman. Obviously he had felt nothing of the turmoil he had caused in her own breast; making hearts flutter must merely be one of the tricks of a libertine's trade.

"I will wait for you, *mon cher*. We will have all the night together. But before you go now, kiss me again!"

Amanda could stand to hear no more. She jumped to her feet and fled, heedless of the crackling of the bushes as she brushed past. Finding Louis as quickly as she could, she pleaded a headache, and after observing the whiteness of her face, he was instantly solicitous. He made their farewells and within minutes they were back in the carriage, on their way home.

When they arrived, Amanda felt a twinge of remorse at having spoiled Louis's pleasure on her account, and she urged him to return to the party. He agreed with only a small show of reluctance, admitting that he had struck up a promising acquaintance with a wealthy young widow. In her assumed role as younger sister, Amanda simply laughed and sped him on his way with a few encouraging words.

But as she lay in her bed, she found herself cursing all men. Louis, who had been so kind to her, was nonetheless a cold-blooded fortune hunter. And Nick! Nick was unspeakable. She felt hot tears pricking her eyelids, and hugged herself tightly under the covers. He was cruel, selfish, and insulting . . . and yet, in the brief minutes when he had held her in his arms, he had made her feel something she had never experienced before, and was hesitant to name.

Oh, yes, she had loved Peter, but looking back upon it now, she realized that she had felt towards him much as she now felt towards Louis. She had felt affection and loyalty, and she had been innocent enough to believe that that was true love, and that nothing more existed between a man and a woman.

Now she knew differently. Ironically, despite their pretended relationship, there was nothing sisterly about her feelings for Nick. When he entered a room, his presence commanded all of her senses; when he looked at her, she felt as if her whole soul were drawn up into her eyes. And when he touched her—no, she could not deny it. She felt wanton with the desire to return the touch, a hundredfold.

Even in the darkness, her cheeks flushed hot with shame. How could she have so little self-control? Was she simply like an animal, lusting after him, just as he was lusting after Liliane Demorest?

No, there was undoubtedly more to it than that. She wanted more than his touch; she wanted his caress, his approval, his admiration. When he had held her, she had had a momentary illusion of feeling wanted and cherished. That illusion, however, had been cruelly shattered. He had embraced her and felt nothing; or, if he had felt any emotion, it was idle contempt. But fool that she was, she still wanted him, desired him, ached for him. Heaven help her, she loved him.

But it was hopeless, truly hopeless. He had shown her often enough that he considered her only a burden. If she were ever to reveal her love for him, he would only use that precious information to wound her. Her only hope was to maintain the shield of indifference towards him—and to find a way to depart his company before he discovered her secret. During the long sleepless hours of that night, Amanda pondered her situation until at long last, she formulated a plan of action.

There was no time to be wasted putting it into effect, and at breakfast the next morning, she cheerfully announced her intention to do more shopping. There was only Louis to ask, of course; *Tante* Sophie never appeared at breakfast, and Nick was presumably still in bed, although Amanda knew that in all likelihood the bed was not his own. Perhaps it was poetic justice, for his deplorable habits would, if she were fortunate, allow her the freedom to escape him.

As expected, Louis offered only amiable approval as she left the house on foot, accompanied only by her maid. After that, it was almost too easy. It was only a few minutes' walk to the shops in the Rue Saint Denis, and when they arrived, Amanda paused before the window of a well-known milliner and turned to face her young maid.

"Poor Martine," she sighed sympathetically. "There's so much I wish to look at here, I know I shall be delayed at least an hour. Why don't you go off and amuse yourself, and meet me here later?"

The young girl's reaction was a comical mixture of delight and dismay. "But mademoiselle, I must not! I should stay here with you, or Monsieur le Comte will be very angry with me!"

"He shall never know," Amanda reassured. "And besides, I think you deserve a brief holiday." She pressed a coin into the girl's hand. "Here, take this, and buy yourself some new ribbons."

The money put an end to all argument; it was simply too good an offer to resist. So, after a minute wasted in listening to Martine's effusive thanks, Amanda was soon left standing alone.

It was a simple matter to locate a cabriolet for hire, and though the driver looked at her somewhat askance, Amanda managed to maintain an unruffled, slightly haughty demeanor. She directed the driver to take her to the residence of the Baron and Baronesse de Fouchard, and was secretly quite relieved when he simply nodded, urging his horses forwards. That had been her biggest gamble, trusting that a hired driver might know an address which she had no way of discovering herself. She settled back against the cushions, confident now that her plan would succeed.

It was unfortunate that she knew virtually nothing of the man whom her schoolfriend Celia Thornton had married. The union had been arranged by Celia's parents, and the bride and groom had met only twice before the ceremony took place. Afterwards, Amanda had received a few letters, full of enthusiasm and *on-dits* about new acquaintances and the latest fashions, but with almost no reference to Celia's husband Henri. Then the letters had stopped altogether.

"Here you are, mademoiselle," the driver called out, intruding upon Amanda's recollections. As she climbed out of the carriage, however, she found herself in front of what was clearly not a private residence, but a large stone complex, with an immense courtyard visible behind an archway.

The Louvre Palace could be seen not far away, but in contrast to that building's regal splendour, this place had a dirty decrepit air. There were only the imposing stone columns and arches, topped by baroque statuary, to hint of the structure's former glory.

"What is this place?" Amanda asked the driver.

"The Palais-Royal. If you want the Baron de Fouchard, you'll find him in there." The driver jerked his thumb towards the palace, and his eyes flicked over her in an insolent manner. She was oblivious of this, however, as she stared at the building looming before her. Some instinct warned her that caution might be in order.

"Will you wait for me, please?" she asked the driver suddenly. "If I find the Baron, I shall expect to be driven home by his own coachman; but if I do not, I shall need your services."

The man looked down at her in affronted surprise. "Look here," he growled, "you'll not get out of paying me with that trick! I'll have my money now, if you please!"

Amanda was taken aback; why in the world should he expect such shabby behavior? Perhaps he was not as accustomed to dealing with the gentry as she had supposed. "You misunderstand me," she stated firmly. "I'll certainly pay you now." She fumbled for the coins in her reticule, and thrust several at him. "But I would be grateful if you would wait for me, just for twenty minutes. And I will pay you for your lost time."

The driver shrugged; even if this pretty *salope* were lying, she certainly had a persuasive way with her. And besides, the Palais was always a good place to pick up fares. He grudgingly agreed to wait, but insisted upon receiving his payment in advance.

Amanda walked through the arches to find herself in a large courtyard, surrounded on all sides by stone-canopied arcades. Underneath these, there were doorways which obviously led to the private rooms above. Arbitrarily she chose the west side to begin her search, and as she looked about for a porter or servant to assist her, she wondered briefly whether this deserted place could truly be a royal palace, and whether the Baron had some kind of appointment which forced him to live here with his family.

Passing through an open doorway, she suddenly found herself face to face with an elderly man. His face was raddled with dissipation, his eyes were foggy and bloodshot, but otherwise he appeared to be respectable enough.

"Pardon me, monsieur," Amanda began politely, "but I am seeking the Baron de Fouchard. Could you please direct me to where I might find him?"

The elderly man peered at her, swaying slightly, and then emitted a raucous laugh, showing discolored teeth. "Oh, he'll receive you all right, *ma petite. Mordieu*, but Henri has all the luck! Follow me, I'll take you to him."

Amanda felt a growing horror creep over her as she was led through a succession of shabby rooms. There were empty bottles lying everywhere, and the rancid odor of old tobacco, and worse. Some rooms were card rooms; others were bedrooms, where in some cases the beds were still occupied at that hour of the morning. She hastily averted her eyes, reminding herself that connected rooms were a common feature of most older palaces, as she had read. And, of course, privacy could hardly be expected in those circumstances, but even so, her English modesty was deeply offended.

Abruptly her guide stopped, and held open a door, motioning for her to enter. She did so, hiding a shudder of revulsion as she had to pass by the man, feeling his foul breath on her cheek. The door then closed behind her with a loud click.

The room was sparsely furnished, except for a large four-poster, and there was a man in a red silk dressing gown who sat propped against the pillows, sipping a cup of what she supposed must be chocolate. His features were dark and rather coarse, with intense eyes which seemed to devour her as she dropped a hesitant curtsey.

"Are you the Baron de Fouchard?" she asked, nervousness making her voice sound curiously weak in her own ears.

"Yes. And who are you, *ma belle?*" he drawled.

She ought to have felt great relief at thus having found her quarry, but instead she experienced a growing disquiet. "I am a friend of your wife," she began, "and I have come a long way to see her; is she here, please?"

The Baron's eyes narrowed, and his mouth curved into a smile, which made his next words come as a considerable shock. "My dear wife is dead. She died in childbirth three years ago. A great pity, because the child was only a girl."

Amanda's mind reeled at the callous words. What kind of monster had Celia married, that her death could cause him only irritation at being cheated of an heir? And what must Celia have endured before death had released her?

"You had a daughter?" she finally managed. "What became of her? Does she live here with you?"

The Baron made a sound which was not quite a laugh. "Here?" he repeated derisively. "Tell me, little Miss Whatever-your-name-is, does this hellish place look like a nursery? No, she does not; I wouldn't live here myself, if it were not for an unfortunate reverse I suffered recently at the tables. There is another gentleman currently living in my *hotel*; however, I will undoubtedly win it back at our next meeting."

Amanda did her best to hide her rising disgust. "But, Monsieur le Baron," she pursed, "where is your child now?"

The Baron began to look impatient, as if the subject bored him. "I had no use for a girl, so I gave her to the mother of my son. She was glad enough to take the brat, for a price."

"The mother of—but you said—" Amanda suddenly clamped her mouth shut as realization dawned. The Baron was speaking of a mistress, of course. This was clearly the point at which she ought to retreat, but Amanda felt impelled to learn more about the child, the only living reminder of her departed friend. "What is the lady's name, and where may I find her?"

"You want to visit La Duroc? I haven't seen her in years." He leaned forward in the bed, arching one black eyebrow. "But I do not think you came here to the Palais-Royal merely to chat. May I guess the real reason why you wished to see me?"

Amanda recoiled before the obvious lechery in his voice, but before she could protest, the door opened, and a woman walked in. It was a woman such as Amanda had never seen before, but no explanations were necessary for her to know exactly who and what the creature was. From the dyed hair and painted face to the slatternly gown, she was a pathetic and terrifying sight.

As soon as she saw Amanda, a stream of words poured out of her mouth which were not familiar to Amanda's French vocabulary. It was easy enough, however, to understand the tone of vicious abuse. For a brief instant Amanda stood transfixed by shock, but then the coarse shouts galvanized her into motion, and she bolted through the door and fled back the same way she had come.

Mercifully she passed unmolested, arriving breathlessly a few moments later at the still-deserted courtyard. Oh, please, she prayed as she ran, let the driver still be there!

But the street was empty.

Chapter Seven

Amanda could have wept with frustration as she stood upon the deserted pavement. How would she ever return to the milliner's in time to meet her maid? If Martine were to panic, and rush home to raise an alarm, Amanda's unexplained absence would only arouse the worst of Nick's suspicions. What was more, the poor girl would probably be sacked.

There was no help for it but to begin walking, and that she did. But so engrossed was she in catching her breath and trying to collect her scattered thoughts, that after walking only a few hundred yards, she failed to notice a large crack in the pavement.

Down she went, as a sharp pain shot through her twisted ankle, and her outstretched hands scraped the cobbled stones. This was simply the final straw, and she collapsed upon the pavement as tears of mingled pain and misery welled into her eyes. For a moment she made no attempt to rise, but simply knelt there, pressing her fists against her forehead while a single, quite unladylike word escaped her lips.

"*Pardon, mamselle, mais—mais—*" A young, heavily accented voice rang out suddenly from above her. Amanda peeked out from under her lashes, in no little embarrassment, and saw a neatly dressed gentleman in a small curricle. He was staring down at her in obvious concern.

"*Je veux*—eh, *je vois*—oh, curse it all!" he stammered. "*Est-ce que*—"

Having risen carefully to her feet, Amanda took pity on his stumbling efforts, and gave him a rather watery smile. "Pray don't distress yourself on my account, sir. I am English."

"You are? Oh, thank heavens!" he exclaimed with relief. "Can't seem to get my tongue round that accursed lingo they speak here. But see here, ma'am, I saw you take that nasty spill just now. Are you all right?"

"Yes, of course," she asserted bravely, testing her weight upon the injured foot. "I really didn't— Ow!" An involuntary cry of pain escaped her and she tottered briefly.

"Wait a moment, ma'am, I'll be right there!" In a flurry of movement, the young man wound his reins tightly around the whipstand, leaped down from the curricle, and rushed up to Amanda. Before she knew what he was about, he had swept her up in his arms. But then, a look of consternation slowly spread over his face; it was quite obvious that once the injured damsel was in his arms, he had no idea what to do next.

Amanda suppressed a smile, seeing the confusion upon the young face so near to hers. Instead, she managed to address him with admirable calm. "It really is not necessary to carry me, sir," she reproved gently. "It was only a small spasm, and I'm certain it will pass quickly."

"Nonsense," the young man replied briskly, recovering some of his aplomb. "It may be broken, at the very least! You must allow me to drive you home."

Since he showed no inclination to put her down, Amanda decided not to argue, especially as they were beginning to attract a number of curious eyes. "Very well, then, sir," she acquiesced. "If you insist, I will accept your kind offer."

Looking quite pleased with himself, he bore her to his carriage, depositing her upon the seat with great care, as though she were a fragile piece of porcelain. Then he swung himself up beside her. "I will gladly take you anywhere, ma'am. Your wish is my command!"

Amanda perceived that her benefactor was younger than she had thought at first, perhaps about eighteen years of age. It was also obvious that he possessed a vididly romantic imagination, and she could not be so cruel as to mock his efforts at chivalry.

"You are very kind, sir," she responded with equal seriousness. "I would be most grateful if you would convey me to the Rue Saint Denis."

He nodded, urging his horses forward, but then abruptly he pulled back on the reins. "Egad! I don't know where it is!" he confessed. "Do you?"

"Why—no!" They looked at each other in disbelief, and then simultaneously began to laugh.

"As a knight in shining armour, you rather leave something to be desired," Amanda could not help teasing.

"I know, I know," he admitted sheepishly. "I never could get things right. Why, at Oxford, I couldn't even climb out my window one night without landing smack on top of the Bagwig's wife's cat. Lord, you never heard such a screeching!"

As they started off once more—now in search of someone to give them directions—Amanda's companion kept her engaged in a lively, though somewhat one-sided conversation. She found him to be a good-natured, voluble young man, whose high spirits had led him more than once into trouble; he had in fact been rusticated for the remainder of his Oxford term, on account of that hapless encounter with the cat.

The brief journey was thus accomplished in a most amiable fashion, their having stopped only twice to seek directions, and having taken a minimum of wrong turns. Nevertheless, it wanted only a few minutes to the hour when they finally arrived in the Rue Saint Denis. By this time there was no more than a slight stiffness in Amanda's ankle, and she laughingly refused the young man's offer to carry her again. She did, however, accept his helping hand as she descended from the high seat.

He retained her hand for a moment longer than necessary, and it was clear that he had something momentous upon his mind. Amanda waited in encouraging silence, aware that an abrupt dismissal would wound the young man's fragile pride.

"I say," he burst out at last. "I know this isn't proper and all that, but my name's Wilbur Smithies. I just wanted you to know."

Amanda could not resist this engaging introduction. "I'm very pleased to meet you, Mr. Smithies. My name is—" She caught herself up only just in time. "Amanda Malvern."

He favored her with a respectful bow. "May I—er, may I call upon you, Miss Malvern?" he asked, somewhat hesitantly.

"Oh, no!" was her quite involuntary exclamation, but then she perceived the crestfallen look upon his face, and hastened to temper the harshness of her words. "I mean—that would be delightful, but I am staying here in the company of my elder brother, and he's dreadfully strict. I'm afraid he would never allow me to receive you on such short acquaintance."

Mr. Smithies seemed mollified, though still regretful. "A real dragon, eh?"

"Yes, indeed," Amanda sighed with utter sincerity. "And besides, it would be so awkward to explain how I came to be alone, without my maid. In fact, I would be most grateful if you—"

"Oh, mum's the word," Mr. Smithies interrupted, favoring her with a conspiratorial wink. "I know how these rigs are run. Not that I can say as how I'd blame him, with someone as pretty as you," he added gallantly. "But I'll not say goodbye just as yet, Miss Malvern. Better as these Frenchies say, *au revoir!*" With a friendly wave of his hand, he climbed back into his vehicle, tipped his hat in her direction, and drove off at a smart pace.

Amanda's smile lingered as his phaeton drove out of sight. Then she glanced sharply at her image in a nearby shop window, tugging her bonnet into place and smoothing the creases from her dress before Martine should appear.

It was not until much later, when Amanda had retired to her room to rest before supper, that she was able to give free rein to her busy thoughts. The day certainly had been one of shocks, she reflected. First she had learned of her friend's death, and obvious suffering at the hands of the lascivious brute who had been her husband. She had also seen firsthand a mode of life with which most well-brought-up young ladies were mercifully unfamiliar.

More immediately, her one real hope of escaping from Nick had turned to dust. Not only did she have no one with whom to take refuge, but her vague notions of taking flight and braving the world alone now seemed ludicrous in the extreme. She shuddered as she recalled the women of the Palais-Royal, women who had had nowhere to turn but to the streets for their very survival. And she might still have been wandering the streets of Paris herself, facing who knows what dangers, if not for the timely intervention of Mr. Smithies. She closed her eyes with a sigh; most likely she would never see him again, but she would always count him as a friend.

And though her own situation must remain unresolved at present, something might yet be done about Celia's child, unwanted and forgotten. Surely there must be a means of helping that unfortunate creature, and Amanda determined to find a way before long.

The next few days passed in a flurry of social calls and parties, following hard upon Amanda's success at the *soirée*. Once or twice *Tante* Sophie bestirred herself to attend, but most often Amanda was escorted only by her official brother and cousin. Among her most frequent gentleman callers was Philippe de Colombe, whose earnest youthful admiration she dismissed as of no consequence, but there were others as well whose effusive flattery was beginning to wear thin upon her patience. It was therefore a most gratifying surprise when, one fine morning, a visitor should be announced as none other than Mr. Smithies.

It so happened that Nick was at that moment on his way out for a drive, and he paused in the foyer to inspect this young Englishman inquiring after Miss Malvern. Before any introduction could be made, however, Miss Malvern herself appeared on the stair, breaking into a smile as soon as she saw her visitor. "Why, Mr. Smithies!" she exclaimed. "How very nice to see you again!"

The unconcealed pleasure in Amanda's voice brought Nick's hard stare to linger upon her face. "I hate to interrupt this touching reunion," Nick broke in, in that soft drawl which Amanda had learned to beware. "But might I ask, who is this

141

fellow, and how comes he to know where you live?"

Amanda hastened to reply, if only to one part of this inquiry. "Nick, this is Mr. Wilbur Smithies, Mr. Smithies, my brother Sir Nicholas Malvern." The two men shook hands with cool politeness, and Mr. Smithies himself then spoke up.

"How d'ye do, sir," he bowed respectfully, in a tone which made Nick feel older than Methuselah. "Beg your pardon for such an irregular visit, but you see, yesterday morning I wasn't looking out, and I rather crashed into your sister in a shop. I'm afraid I made both of us drop our loot. Then, when I got home, I saw . . ." With a dramatic flourish, he drew a small wrapped packet out from under his coat. ". . . that I'd snagged one of her parcels by mistake! So naturally, first thing today I got her address from the shop, so I could return the lady's rightful property, and make the apologies, you know."

At this point in his narrative, he favored Amanda with a small wink, causing her to utter a faint choking sound, which she immediately concealed by bursting into speech. "Oh, how very kind of you, sir! I'll own that I had not noticed anything missing until I returned home, and I had feared my combs lost in the street, and gone forever. Please, Nick, may I offer Mr. Smithies a cup of tea, in thanks for his trouble?"

Nick's manner softened slightly. Mr. Smithies resembled nothing so much at that moment as an eager young pup wagging its tail ever so slightly, uncertain of acceptance but nevertheless hopeful.

"Certainly you may, Amanda. I'm afraid I have an appointment for which I am already late, but I think no one will mind if we dispense with the proprieties for once." He reached down from his superior height to shake Mr. Smithies's hand briefly, and then took his leave, favoring Amanda only with an amused glance.

Amanda let out a long sigh of admiration as she ushered Mr. Smithies into the parlour and rang for a servant to bring their tea. "How did you discover where I lived?" she inquired.

Mr. Smithies shook his head in mock reproof. "You're a dashed sight too modest, Miss Malvern. I merely asked a question here and there, and *voilà!*"

"You're a marvel," she congratulated him. "But however did you think of all that nonsense about a parcel?"

He preened a bit. "Thought it was good stuff, myself. You see, I knew there must be some way to see you, despite that brother of yours. And though he's younger than I thought, I must say he's every bit as cool a customer as you said!" Then a slow grin spread over his face. "Only it's a good thing he didn't ask to see what was in that parcel of yours."

"Why not?" Amanda inquired, upon which he handed it to her, and she proceeded to unwrap a half-dozen plump cigars. Their laugher echoed through the house for a long time afterwards.

In the days that followed, Amanda's social schedule was full, and with Nick most often serving as her escort, she had the opportunity to see more sides of his character. Though he could certainly be rude and selfish on occasion, when he was on his best behaviour in public, it was easy to imagine the trail of broken hearts he must have left behind him. His manner was slightly aloof in general, but when he smiled directly into a woman's eyes, his charm was impossible to resist.

And he in his turn appeared to be gentling towards her, tolerating her presence with less irritation, and even seeming to enjoy her conversation. Despite the disparity between their social backgrounds, Amanda discovered that they had many interests in common, and although Nick still clung to his low opinion of women in general, he unconsciously treated her as an equal. Amanda had almost begun to hope that he had forgotten his scheme of marrying her off to the highest bidder.

As it was, it was difficult to brood over her long-range prospects, when there was a more immediate problem at hand: the growing depth of her feelings for Nick. Despite her efforts to be rational where he was concerned, his mere presence was sufficient to threaten her composure, and her treacherous heart continued to betray her every time she saw his face or heard his voice. Whenever Nick walked into a room, she could feel the color mounting in her cheeks and the quickened beat of her pulse. It was as though he made her come alive in a way she had never experienced, mentally as well as physically. There was little she could do, however, but conceal her reactions as best she could, until fate should bring about some change in her present situation.

It was not long before a turn of events came, at a cotillion held at the magnificent town house of the Comte and Comtesse de Mornay. Amanda's popularity was by now well established, and after a succession of dances, it was with relief that she discovered the next one promised to Philippe de Colombe. Begging his indulgence, she pleaded fatigue, and asked to sit out the dance in his company. Philippe agreed, manfully concealing his disappointment, and upon her request, he departed in search of refreshments.

Amanda was left alone for a moment, grateful to catch her breath, but she was not to be allowed more than an instant's peace. In a cloud of rustling silks and perfume, Madame Demorest swept up to her and laid a hand insistently upon her arm.

"Oh, you are alone, *ma petite!* How pretty you are tonight!" The woman's smile did not reach the coldness of her eyes. "There is someone you must meet, someone very handsome and very rich. Come with me!"

Before Amanda could utter a word of protest, she found herself being towed towards the buffet, where a large man stood slightly apart from the others. He turned as Madame Demorest approached; somehow the woman had the uncanny ability to make her presence felt. Or perhaps it was just the use of too much perfume, Amanda thought wickedly.

"Here she is, *mon cher* Baron, the lovely Miss

145

Amanda Malvern. Miss Malvern, this is Henri, Baron de Fouchard, who has been simply mad to meet you!"

Amanda's heart received a nasty jolt as she recognized the very man whom she least wished to see. Now able to view him at closer range, she observed that he was about forty years of age, thick-set, with curling black hair slightly touched with gray at the temples, and heavy brows that framed deep-set dark eyes. He was well-dressed in an ostentatious style, with a large diamond pin sparkling in his cravat, and rings upon the fleshy hand he extended towards her. It was obvious that somehow the Baron had managed to repair his financial fortunes—and from his smug expression, it was equally obvious that he recognized her as his visitor from the Palais-Royal, although she could only pray he would refrain from revealing that fact.

There was no choice but to extend her own hand politely, dropping a slight curtsey, but instead of the usual brushing of fingers, the Baron clasped her hand in a strong grip and bent forward to press a kiss upon her knuckles. His lips were hot and moist, and Amanda's smile froze as she experienced an instinctive shudder of revulsion. After an instant, however, he let go of her, and his manner became correct once more.

"It is so great a pleasure to meet you, Mademoiselle," he said in his languid, slightly gruff voice. "I have been away from Paris, and when I saw you tonight, I knew that I had to meet you. Will you honor me with this dance?"

Amanda was aware of Madame Demorest hovering in the background with an enigmatic smile upon her face. "I am flattered, Monsieur," Amanda responded with frigid politeness. "But I am afraid that my dances for this evening are already promised. If you will excuse me, I must return to my partner now."

With another quick curtsey, she retreated rapidly to where she could see a bewildered Philippe wandering through the crowd. Behind her, however, she heard the echo of the Baron's voice. "Utterly charming, Liliane. You have chosen well."

Early the next morning, a footman entered the breakfast parlour, bearing a note upon a silver tray. Louis tore it open with curiosity.

"Aha. It is from Liliane. She proposes a riding excursion to the Bois de Boulogne this Saturday, with a luncheon *al fresco*."

Nick uttered a short, mirthless laugh. "I should hardly think Liliane the type to enjoy anything so fatiguing."

"You have reason, my friend," Louis agreed, "but such parties are all the rage this season. And Liliane is never out of the mode."

"Well, in any case, Amanda won't go; we haven't time to give her riding lessons."

"I beg your pardon!" Amanda interrupted, her pride affronted. "I can ride perfectly well, thank you, even without your instructions!"

Nick eyed her skeptically. "I dislike taking

chances, especially when appearances are of the first importance."

Amanda's eyelids flickered briefly, as his words reminded her of the masquerade in which they were embroiled. Louis, however, rose quickly to her defense. "But, my friend, do not be so harsh," he protested. "I am certain that your sister rides like an angel. And in any case, Liliane will have eyes only for you."

Nick merely shrugged, acknowledging this praise with an indifference which made Amanda long to slap him. "Very well, Louis, we shall go. But I rely upon you to help me see that Amanda stays out of trouble."

"That will be a great pleasure," Louis said gallantly, giving Amanda a friendly wink. It was some time, however, before her irritation dissipated. Let us wait until Saturday, she thought, and you will both see whether or not I can ride!

The day of the excursion dawned bright and clear, and Amanda rose with a sense of pleasurable anticipation. She cared nothing for the party itself, but it had been such a long time since she had been able to ride! As the maid brushed Amanda's hair to a shining burnished bronze, her mind drifted back to the days when she and Peter would ramble over the countryside, mounted on two of the Squire's best bloods.

With a twinge of surprise, she realized that in thinking of Peter, she no longer felt pain, but only a fond memory of the happy times they had shared. It was as if Peter's ghost were finally laid to rest, after all the years of grieving. Or was it that Peter's image merely paled, driven out of Amanda's heart by a new and far more disturbing presence? Resolutely she curbed her wayward thoughts, concentrating once more upon her toilette. Fancying herself in love with Nick was an inexcusable folly, and the sooner she got over it, the better off she would be!

She descended the stairs to find the gentlemen waiting in the foyer. Louis smiled appreciatively at Amanda's riding habit of deep red velvet, which enhanced the golden color of her eyes, and hugged the graceful curves of her figure. Her neatly coiled hair was hidden under a hat, which sported small plumes carefully dyed to match. The effect was very elegant indeed, but instead of appreciation it brought a speculative frown to Nick's brow. She was becoming far too sophisticated in her mode of dress, he was reflecting, concerned lest she betray her true age and maturity; to Amanda, however, his seeming disapproval fell like a blow upon her bruised heart. She turned away, striving to smile at Louis as he offered his escort towards the waiting horses.

The mount saddled for her was a spirited mare, and Louis experienced a moment's uncertainty. It was the tamest horse in his stables, but still it was far from docile. As soon as Amanda was mounted, however, he breathed in relief as he saw the expert way in which she handled the reins, and the ease with which she controlled the horse's restless prancing.

Nick also watched, and as Amanda's control became apparent he slowly relaxed, only belatedly aware that his every nerve had been tensed for a quick rescue. After a few moments, he turned to his own horse, but not before allowing his gaze to rest upon Amanda with unwilling admiration.

As they approached the park where the party was supposed to assemble, Amanda saw that in place of a large group as expected, there were only three persons, with a single servant at a discreet distance. Amanda recognized Madame Demorest, and also the young widow whom Louis had been pursuing; to her dismay, she then saw that the third person was Baron de Fouchard.

"Good morning, Nicholas!" Liliane trilled, her voice echoing in the thin morning air. "How very like you to keep us waiting, *mon cher!* I believe you know Madame Rouget; and this is Henri, Baron de Fouchard. I warn you," she added teasingly, "he is a devoted admirer of your sister."

"How do you do, Sir Nicholas," the Baron intoned, bowing slightly. He was mounted on a huge gray stallion, which chafed at a tight bit; Amanda found her distaste for the man only increased by his subtle cruelty.

Nick gave a curt reply, his pale eyes meeting the Baron's black ones for a moment as they silently assessed each other. Then Nick turned aside with an indifferent shrug, shifting his attention to Liliane. The Baron's eyes gleamed for an instant with what might have been satisfaction, before regaining their expression of bland placidity.

The party started off in a westerly direction, and it was not long before they reached the outskirts of the city. In the open space, the group separated almost immediately into three pairs, and Amanda perceived with a sinking heart that she was to be linked with the Baron. This had obviously been planned by Madame Demorest, but to what end, Amanda could not quite fathom. Unfortunately matters soon became clear, as the Baron initiated a determined courtship. He asked Amanda incessant questions, which she did her best to evade, and paid her overblown compliments which she simply ignored. Occasionally she attempted to pursue a neutral topic of conversation, but the Baron refused to be diverted. He seemed to be especially pleased to hear that she had not yet made an official debut, and that Nick was her sole guardian in Paris.

After a journey which seemed interminable, the party finally reached an attractive glade within the Bois de Boulogne, the huge park which had reached the heights of fashion before the war. Madame Demorest announced that luncheon would be served. Before she could dismount, Amanda found the Baron's hands, around her waist, lifting her down from her horse. Amanda's fists clenched as he begged her pardon for the liberty, a smirk upon his fleshy lips; she simply nodded, not trusting herself to speak. She made sure, however, to seat herself at some distance from the Baron as the food was laid out upon a cloth.

The luncheon was simple but delicious, with several courses appearing mysteriously out of the servant's two large baskets. There was cold pheasant and duckling, roast beef, dressed crab and lobster patties, and an array of fruits and small cakes for dessert. There was also a considerable quantity of wine, which Amanda partook of sparingly. The others, however, were less restrained, especially the Baron, whose face soon became unattractively flushed.

It was more than two hours later when the party finally decided to turn homeward. Returning from the small thicket where the ladies had retired to freshen up, Amanda found the Baron waiting to assist her to mount. There was no polite way to avoid the situation, and Amanda had to bear with it, merely gritting her teeth as she placed her foot within his tight grasp.

They set out once more, and this time the couples separated almost immediately. Emboldened by the effects of the wine, Louis and his widow turned their horses down a side path, and dropped entirely from sight. Then, a few moments later, Madame Demorest issued a laughing challenge to Nick, to race towards a fence which was barely visible in the distance. Nick, who was by this time heartily bored, lost no time in accepting the dare, and the two spurred their horses forward, soon disappearing over a small ridge.

Anxious not to be left behind with the Baron, Amanda urged her own horse to a gallop, but after only a few hundred feet she felt a violent lurching sensation. With horror, she realized that the saddle girth had broken, as she felt herself tumbling helplessly to the ground.

She opened her eyes a few moments later, feeling dazed but unhurt. Somehow she had landed in a bed of thick weeds which had cushioned her fall;

and then she also remembered that in the instant when the saddle broke, the Baron had been beside her, tugging upon her horse's reins. When her horse had slowed, the momentum of her impact was lessened; but how had the Baron come to be there, at the exact right moment?

Amanda struggled to sit up, and found that her shoulders were cradled in a large, strong arm. "Do not move, my dear. You must rest." The Baron's voice as loud in her ear, and his breath was hot upon her cheek. Revulsion washed over her, at the fact that she was lying in this man's arms, and with an effort she managed to twist out of his grasp, regaining her feet unsteadily. She had to lean against a nearby tree, for the sudden movement had made her head begin to spin in an alarming fashion.

The Baron was watching her with glittering eyes, as if her resistance were somehow whetting his interest in her. "Do not be concerned for the proprieties, my dear. I deplore this terrible accident, but since you are not injured, I cannot help being glad that fate has thrown us alone together once more."

She regarded him warily as he continued, still crouched upon one knee before her. "As you know, my sweet, I no longer have a wife. It is past time that I remarry, and I have been looking for just such a one as you—young, innocent, and willing to conform herself to my particular . . . requirements."

"You have not found her, Monsieur. I do not wish to marry you, and I beg you as a gentleman to say no more." Amanda strove to maintain at least the appearance of civility, although her voice betrayed a trace of the disgust which this proposal had inspired.

The Baron merely smiled. "On the contrary, my dear. You have no say in the matter. You see, I have known men such as your brother. They care nothing for anyone but themselves, and your pleas will fall on deaf ears. What will matter to him is the fact that by the time he realizes something is wrong, and returns to find you, you will be in a . . . shall we say, compromising situation." He laughed, an unpleasant sound. "Your dear brother will insist that I marry you, regardless of your own wishes."

The import of his words slowly sank into her whirling head, and Amanda's eyes widened in dismay as the Baron rose to his feet and started to approach her.

"Don't come near me!" she gasped, shrinking against the tree; and then she realized that somehow her riding crop was still gripped tightly in her hand. With a swift movement, she whipped it hard against his face.

The Baron cried out in pain, falling backward a few steps as he clutched his cheek. A long red slash was oozing blood. "You stupid bitch!" he hissed. "I was only going to kiss you. But now—"

Before she could strike him again, he shot out a hand and wrenched her wrist in a painful grip, forcing her to release the riding crop. It fell harmlessly upon the grass, as the Baron seized Amanda's shoulders and drew her hard against him.

A quarter of a mile away, Nick patted his horse absently, a slight frown creasing his brow. "Where the devil are they?" he asked Liliane. "They ought to have been right behind us."

She gave a little laugh, tossing her dusky curls. "Are you so unhappy to be alone with me, Nicholas? Let us leave them behind," she coaxed. "We have so little time to be together, you and I."

Her words seemed to have made no impression upon him, as he continued to stare at the empty ridge behind them. "I don't care for her to be compromised," he replied shortly. "I'd better go and have a look."

"Well! And if she is compromised?" Liliane snapped impatiently. "Then she must be wed, and you shall have no more worry about her. And then we can be together, as we have been before!"

At these words, Nick turned his head and gave her a long deliberate look. "And did you perhaps arrange this with your friend the Baron?" he asked, very softly.

Liliane shrugged, pouting her lips seductively. "And so? He is mad for the child. And he is very rich, with a good name. What more could she want?" She glanced at him from beneath her lashes, but shrank back involuntarily as she saw the expression on his face.

His eyes were as cold as chips of green ice, and when he spoke, the soft drawl did little to mask his anger. "You will learn, Liliane, that I dislike having my hand forced." Abruptly he wheeled his horse back in the direction of the opposite ridge, urging it to a canter, while Madame Demorest desperately called out his name.

First anger, and then fear lent strength to Amanda as she struggled against the Baron's attack, kicking and writhing to escape his fierce embrace. Her efforts had little effect, however, seeming only to arouse him further. With a muttered laugh he pinned her back against the tree.

"Petite salaude," he muttered thickly. "You'll be grateful to be wed to any man, once I've finished with you."

"No, never!" she defied him hoarsely, her strength ebbing. "I'll see you hang for this, you—" Her words were cut off by a powerful slap against her cheek, knocking her head back sharply and drowning her in a temporary wave of faintness.

"What the hell is going on here?" At the sound of Nick's angry voice, the Baron looked up sharply, and let go of Amanda, who sagged against the tree trunk. He watched through narrowed eyes as Nick dismounted and strode towards him with clenched fists.

The Baron bowed, seeking to recover an air of aplomb. "I fear you have found us out, Sir Nicholas. Your sister and I have just reached an understanding, and I'm afraid we allowed our passion to overcome our good judgment. But believe me, I am as anxious as you to avoid scandal, and I am quite prepared to marry her as soon as can be arranged."

Nick checked his stride in surprise, but his jaw tightened as he took in Amanda's drooping form and the bloody weal on the Baron's cheek. "Your lovemaking seems to lack a certain finesse," he replied contemptuously. "I believe you'll have to look elsewhere for a bride."

"Oh, I think not, Sir Nicholas," the Baron countered with arrogant confidence. "I might be forgetful enough to mention the delight of your sister's kisses to a few of my friends, and that is something I am certain you would wish to avoid."

"You underestimate me, Baron," Nick said with dangerous calm. "Before you threaten scandal, consider how it will sound when *I* regale your acquaintances with the tale of the little plot hatched between you and Liliane. Oh, yes, I know all about it. My sister's reputation will survive, but I fear yours may not." The Baron lost some of his smugness as Nick continued. "Come to think of it . . ." With a deadly smile, he drew his small silver-mounted pistol from the pocket of his coat. "I believe her reputation might even survive the scandal of your death—by my hand."

The Baron seemed to shrink visibly as he fell back a step, and then scrambled hastily towards his horse. He swung himself into the saddle and dug his spurs into his mount as it bolted forward; horse and rider crashed through the thicket and rapidly disappeared from sight.

The painful sparks slowly receded, and Amanda became aware of her head throbbing painfully, and someone holding her shoulders, calling her name.

"No, no," she moaned, trying to turn her head away; but then her face was seized between two strong hands.

"Amanda, it's me, Nick. The Baron is gone, and you're safe now. Wake up, darling, please!"

With a tremendous effort, Amanda opened her eyes to see Nick's face hovering close to hers. To her utter amazement, she saw that his expression held not anger but tender concern, and uncontrollably her eyes welled with tears. His response was to gather her up in his arms, stroking her hair and murmuring words of comfort. Amanda did not care that his feelings were those of sympathy, and nothing more; for the moment, she was content merely to be held close to him.

After a short while, Amanda recovered herself sufficiently to be able to push away from the haven of Nick's arms and dash the tears out of her eyes. If she allowed herself to cling to him, he might soon guess the true nature of her feelings. "I beg your pardon, Nick," she said, her voice still slightly choked. "I'm not very brave."

"The devil you're not," he replied tersely. "From the look of his face, you were putting up quite a fight. Now, do you mind telling me just what happened?"

She drew a deep breath. "We were racing to catch up with you, and then suddenly I fell off my horse. My saddle girth broke—I think he may have cut it." Nick's brows drew together sharply. "Then when I was on the ground, he said he wanted to marry me. I refused, and that's when he tried to—" Her voice faltered, and Nick pulled her once more into his arms, this time pressing her head to his shoulder.

"But he didn't, and that's all that matters. It's over now." His hold tightened almost painfully, and for a few moments she drowned in the blissful warmth.

As he held her against him, Nick was taken aback by the rush of emotion he felt. Anger at the Baron still burned hotly within him, but this was something else. It was more than protectiveness, and more than simple concern; and it definitely had to do with Amanda. Nor was this feeling merely one of desire, though Nick was fully conscious of the soft curves of Amanda's body as she drew strength from the hard circle of his arms. Whatever it was, he did not wish for it; Amanda was going to pass in and out of his life just like the other women he had known, and by his own preference. He had no wish for the kind of commitments that women seemed to demand, and least of all did he care for the unsettling effect Amanda was beginning to have upon his equanimity.

With unexpected abruptness, he released her and stepped back, frowning slightly. "Are you able to travel?" he asked curtly, and the tenderness Amanda thought she had heard in his voice earlier might never have existed.

Or, it was even more likely that he had never felt any such tenderness at all, and her overwrought emotions had caused her to imagine something which did not exist. That painful suspicion seemed to be well-founded as Nick strode towards his horse and seized its bridle, leading it to where she stood. There was no trace of gentleness in his firm grip as he boosted her into the saddle, and then swung himself up behind her. As they moved forward, with Amanda's mount trotting close behind, she felt the hard tension of his body, and was reminded of their first contact on the night she had been abducted. At that unhappy memory, she had to struggle against fresh tears. It seemed like so long ago, and so much had changed since then . . . except for Nick, who, in spite of his brief flashes of humanity, remained as aloof and inscrutable as ever before.

Chapter Eight

Amanda's unpleasant encounter with the Baron was not without its repercussions. Aside from the Baron's unexplained absence from a number of social events, the incident appeared to have caused an irreparable split between Nick and Liliane Demorest. Amanda could scarcely help feeling considerable relief upon both counts.

At the same time, however, her mind became more and more troubled over the unknown fate of Celia's child. Now aware of the Baron's cruelty at first hand, Amanda began to fear that the child might be brutally abused, if indeed she still lived.

Not one to tarry once her mind was made up, upon the first occasion when Nick and Louis were both absent, and *Tante* Sophie enjoying the afternoon siesta which could on no account ever be disturbed, Amanda summoned Louis's closed travelling coach. Her previous experience with hired carriages had been more than sufficient, and besides, she reasoned, she had no cause to fear the servants' indiscretion. Nonetheless, she prudently donned a veil before departing the house.

After instructing the coachman to take her to the Hotel Fouchard, a newly repossessed town house of which the Baron had boasted in great detail, Amanda pondered her next step. Above all, it was imperative to learn the whereabouts of this Mademoiselle Duroc, the woman who was the only clue to the child. Such an inquiry, however, would have to be conducted with the utmost discretion.

Amanda did not therefore descend from the coach until the driver, at her request, had ascertained that the Baron was out. Thus given the all-clear, she mounted the steps with a purposeful tread, and announced to a rather surprised *maître d'hôtel* that she wished to have a private word with the housekeeper.

When ushered into the lady's presence, Amanda forced herself to ignore the dour scrutiny with which she was being subjected from head to toe. Instead, she calmly removed her gloves and addressed the woman in French.

"Forgive me for this intrusion, Madame," Amanda begged civilly, "but I have come in search of information, and you, I believe, may be the only person who can help me."

After another suspicious glance, the housekeeper apparently concluded that Amanda was quality after all, and she dipped a halfhearted curtsey. "I promise you nothing," the woman responded grudgingly, "but I will listen. You may sit down, Mademoiselle."

"Thank you." Amanda paused, and then

launched directly into her subject. "My name is not important for you to know, Madame, but I was a very dear friend of your former mistress, the Baronesse. I knew her when she was still Miss Celia Thornton." The housekeeper was visibly startled, but Amanda pressed on. "Since I have arrived in Paris, I have learned that there was a child born to my friend, and given into the care of a certain Mademoiselle Duroc."

The woman gave the slightest of nods.

"Madame, all I ask of you is that you tell me where I may find this woman, so I may see for myself whether the child is well cared for."

Amanda held her breath, in case the woman's loyalties should prove stronger than her willingness to oblige, but there was no refusal. Nor was there any information forthcoming, however, as the housekeeper sat with tightly pursed lips.

Amanda was not unprepared for this reaction. "You see, Madame," she continued smoothly, "I wish only to make sure that Mademoiselle Duroc has sufficient funds to carry out her duties." She drew out a large purse of coins, dangling it nonchalantly before the woman's greedy eyes. "And, of course, I shall be most grateful to you for your assistance."

The prospect of money immediately loosened the woman's tongue. "Very well, Mademoiselle. You will find Mademoiselle Duroc at number twelve, Rue des Bons Enfants. It is a small street just west of the Palais-Royal."

Oh, no, Amanda thought, shivering slightly. Not that place again! But outwardly she remained composed, rising smoothly to her feet. "Thank you, Madame. Pray accept this small token of my gratitude." Amanda placed a handful of gold coins upon a nearby table. "Good day."

As her carriage clattered homewards, Amanda marshalled her mental energies, formulating her next stage of campaign. There was no further doubt in her mind that some action must be taken on behalf of the child, but she knew better than to try and enlist Nick's sympathy for the cause. He had roundly forbidden her to have anything further to do with the Baron, and moreover she knew that he would not countenance her becoming involved in any kind of illegal activity. And it would no doubt be illegal to interfere with how a child was being treated by its natural father, and in a foreign country no less!

Nevertheless, Amanda had a fair notion of a plan of rescue that might work, assuming that Nick and Louis were occupied elsewhere the following day. And assuming as well that she had enough funds to cover the expenses. It was most fortunate that Nick had just given her a rather large sum, intended to cover the purchase of parasols, reticules, and other paraphernalia appropriate to her pretended status. Although Amanda hated to touch that money, knowing that she was sinking deeper and deeper into his debt, at least it would be spent to excellent purpose.

All that remained was to arrange the practical details. After requesting the coachman to be ready once more at ten o'clock the following morning, she went into the house to change for dinner.

Before summoning the maid, however, she sat down to write a letter to Mr. Wilbur Smithies, in care of the Hotel Triomphal.

"I ask your pardon, Monsieur le Comte, but the coachman has asked to have a word with you, in private." The *maître d'hôtel* addressed the gentlemen as they lingered over their brandy; *Tante* Sophie and Amanda had long since retired for the evening.

"Jean-Pierre? What in the world should he want?" Louis exclaimed. "Oh, show him in—and pay no heed to Sir Nicholas here."

"Very well, Monsieur le Comte," the butler bowed respectfully, opening the door to admit a tall man, obviously ill-at-ease, who clutched his tricorned hat tightly before him, and eyed Sir Nicholas hesitantly.

"That will be all," Louis dismissed his *maître d'hôtel*. "Now, Jean-Pierre, what have you to say to me? You may speak freely in front of my guest," he added, following the direction of the coachman's furtive glance.

"It's about the young lady, Monsieur le Comte."

"You mean Miss Malvern?" Louis reacted with surprise. "What is it?"

"Well, you see, Monsieur le Comte," the man stammered. "Today she asked me to drive her, and since you had not forbidden me, I did as she asked."

"What's wrong with that?" Louis queried impatiently.

"It's—*eh bien,* it's where she asked me to take her."

"Well??"

"To the Hotel Fouchard, Monsieur le Comte."

There was a moment's silence, as Louis glanced anxiously at his friend. Nick was silent, his eyes hooded, but there was a tense set to his jaw.

"I thought that you would wish to know this, Monsieur le Comte. And also that she has asked me to drive her again tomorrow morning at ten o'clock. What do you wish me to do, Monsieur le Comte?"

Nick spoke up before Louis could reply. "Your services will not be necessary. I shall drive her myself," he stated calmly in his lightly accented French.

The man looked inquiringly at Louis, who then nodded in confirmation of the order. "Thank you for your vigilance, Jean-Pierre. You shall be rewarded." He waved his hand dismissively, and the man bowed himself out, murmuring thanks.

After he had gone, Louis turned to Nick in bewilderment. "What can she possibly be doing, visiting a man such as the Baron?" he wondered, politely reverting to English.

"I don't know," Nick ground out, showing anger for the first time. "But I assure you, dear Louis, I intend to find out."

Time dragged interminably for Amanda on the following morning, but when ten o'clock finally arrived, it seemed that fate was working entirely in her favor. Both Louis and Nick had been unusually quiet at breakfast, but they excused themselves as expected and left the house well in advance of the crucial hour. When Amanda stepped outside to meet the carriage as she had ordered, she glanced only briefly at the driver, who was well muffled against the chill morning air.

"To the Hotel Triomphal, please," she directed, and then settled back, her body tense with anxiety. She was gambling a great deal upon the strength of Wilbur's chivalrous inclinations, and could only pray that she was not mistaken. The very moment that the carriage drew to a halt in the hotel's paved courtyard, she stepped out, looking about her with worried impatience. Fortunately, however, she had not long to wait.

"Hallo, there, Amanda!" A familiar voice rang out clearly across the courtyard, and Wilbur Smithies came hurrying to her side.

"Oh, but I *am* glad to see you!" she exclaimed, clasping his hand warmly. "I was so afraid you'd not be able to meet me at such short notice!"

"Well, it's a good job your letter arrived so soon, Amanda," he replied. "In fact, I was coming round to see you this afternoon, to tell you that my father wants me home. I'd planned on leaving tomorrow."

"Tomorrow?" Amanda repeated blankly. "You're leaving tomorrow for England? Oh—" Sudden animation leaped into her voice. "Oh, but that's capital! Here, let me explain—and you'd best come into the carriage, where we can speak without fear of eavesdroppers."

With the window shades drawn, their hushed voices could no longer be heard with any clarity, except when Amanda put her head out the window some ten minutes later. "Driver!" she called out cheerfully. "Take us to number twelve, Rue des Bons Enfants."

The coachman did not respond immediately, as if the undesirable address took him by surprise, but then without a word he flicked the reins, and the horses sprang forward.

The neighborhood surrounding the Palais-Royal was only slightly less squalid than the palace itself. Amanda and Wilbur had to pick their way carefully across the muddy, filth-littered street. From windows high above, several persons could be seen peering down, staring at the fine coach and its occupants. When Amanda finally knocked upon the door of number twelve, she was more than grateful to have Wilbur's solid protective presence behind her.

After repeated knockings, the door creaked slowly open to reveal a slatternly young woman of about thirty years of age. Her blond hair was over-crimped, and her dress was a gaudy, cheaply made attempt at high fashion. Her face looked tired and worn, and despite the early hour, her eyes were glazed from what she had already imbibed.

"Are you Mademoiselle Duroc?" Amanda demanded, at which the woman cocked her head slightly in acknowledgment. "I am here to see Mademoiselle de Fouchard. Would you please take me to her?"

"Who?" Mademoiselle Duroc looked blank for a moment. "Oh, you mean that brat." Her bleary eyes focused in suspicion. "Who wants to know?"

All at once Amanda lost patience; she had already seen more than enough. "Come on, Wilbur," she announced determinedly. They pushed their way easily past Mademoiselle Duroc, who was in any case swaying on her feet, and followed a winding staircase to a large room on the first floor. It was dingy and shabbily furnished, but Amanda took little notice of this. Instead, her attention was riveted upon a little girl who sat in one corner, quietly playing with a rag doll.

The child was the living image of Celia, with angelically fair hair and innocent blue eyes. She was small for her age of three years—perhaps because of an inadequate diet—but she appeared to be healthy, and as she crooned to the doll, it seemed that she had a lively spirit which had not yet been quenched. Amanda's heart was torn, however, by the child's dirty and unkempt state.

Amanda approached, giving her a warm smile. *"Bonjour, mignonne,"* she said softly.

The child looked up with wide curious eyes. *"Bonjour,"* she piped.

"Come here, sweetheart," Amanda beckoned. "I'm going to take you for a little trip." She reached out her arms, but the child shrank back in sudden fear.

"Who are you?" she squealed.

"I'm a friend of your *maman*," Amanda reassured. "I promise you, everything will be all right."

"Maman?" the child repeated, suddenly docile as Amanda picked her up. *"Maman!"*

Mademoiselle Duroc suddenly appeared in the

doorway, hands on hips. "What the holy devil is going on here!" she screeched.

The child had no doubt heard every word the woman was about to utter, but with a glance at Wilbur's shocked expression, Amanda decided to forego this new opportunity to enlarge her own vocabulary.

"There's no need to be concerned, Mademoiselle," she interrupted hastily. "We are acting on behalf of the child's parent." But not the one you think, she added to herself grimly. "We are aware that the child has been an unreasonable burden upon you, and we have now made other arrangements for her care. But whatever money the Baron has been sending will continue as before." This seemed to be a safe enough claim, since the Baron would not know that the child had been removed.

"And there is a small token of our gratitude." Amanda pressed a purse into Mademoiselle Duroc's hand, after which the woman stood aside to let them pass, concerned more with counting out the coins than with the departure of her charge. Just before they reached the stairs, however, the woman looked up.

"Here," she said reluctantly. "Take this for the little one—it helps her to sleep." She seized a half-empty bottle of spirits and thrust it out at Amanda.

Despite her initial reaction of distaste, Amanda comprehended swiftly that this was a belated gesture of concern toward the child, expressed in the only way the woman knew how. She therefore accepted the bottle with an understanding nod, handing it silently to her bemused companion.

Moments later, when they reached the street, Wilbur expelled a large sigh of relief. "Whew! That was a nasty business, eh?"

"Yes, but it might have been far worse," she reminded him. "At least the child appears healthy enough."

"*Maman*, where are we going?" the child piped up suddenly.

The coachman dropped his whip with a startling clatter, but Amanda merely cast an annoyed glance in his direction before attending to the squirming little girl in her arms. "Hush, *chérie*, we'll tell you in a moment. Now let's just get into the coach, shall we?"

The next stop was the establishment of a certain clothing merchant in the Rue Grandin, in front of which Amanda descended alone.

"Wait a moment," Wilbur cried out in a slightly panicked tone. "Won't you take her with you?"

"No, why should I?" Amanda replied calmly. "In her present state, she would only attract undesirable attention. Besides, you'd best get used to being alone with her. You'll have her for at least two days, you know!"

"Yes, I certainly do know," Wilbur acknowledged glumly as Amanda disappeared into the shop. "Why did I ever mention that I had young sisters?"

When she returned, however, she was relieved to see that he had established the best of terms with his small companion, dandling her upon his knee and regaling her with stories which she apparently found highly entertaining, despite being unable to understand a single word.

"Driver, back to the Hotel Triomphal, please," Amanda ordered briskly as she reentered the carriage, carrying a large bundle in her arms.

As the carriage rattled over the paving stones, Amanda opened the wrappings to reveal a small portmanteau, filled with dresses, shifts, and other accoutrements of a very young lady of fashion. She proceeded to strip off the child's shabby clothing, and dress her in the new garments, which would be more appropriate for her temporary role as Miss Smithies, Wilbur's niece.

"See here, Amanda, I've just thought of something," Wilbur announced at one point, as Amanda was trying to aim a small foot into an even smaller stocking. "Hadn't we better give her a name?"

"You're quite right," Amanda agreed. She looked down upon the child's blond curls. "She looks like a little angel . . . what about the name Celeste?"

"Jolly good!" Wilbur approved.

"Of course," she admonished, "before we let ourselves be swept away by our enthusiasm, we must remember that Celia's father, Colonel Thornton, may prefer something else. However, that name ought to do for the time being."

Wilbur's expression was suddenly grave. "Amanda, are you quite certain that this Colonel Thornton will be willing to accept the child into his household? The evidence is a bit thin, after all."

"You never saw Celia, or you'd not think such a

172

thing," Amanda answered sadly. "There could be no doubt of her parentage. And besides," she added more briskly, "I recall the Colonel as a loving father, despite being rather a tyrant; I believe he must have regretted arranging a marriage that took his daughter so faraway. It must have been a great sorrow to hear of her death, and if he had any notion of how his grandchild was being treated, he would have taken steps to remove her himself."

Wilbur grimaced. "I must confess, it's not a tale I'd particularly wish to be carrying to an old man."

Amanda pressed his hand reassuringly. "Don't worry, Wilbur, I'd not ask you to be the bearer of such news. I've written him a long letter, which says all he'll need to know, and no more."

Twenty minutes later, the three of them stood together in the cobbled courtyard of the Hotel Triomphal, with a timid Celeste clinging to Wilbur's coattail. Amid the noontime bustle, their words were just barely audible to the coachman hunched forward upon the high carriage seat.

"Dearest Wilbur, I cannot thank you enough for doing this," Amanda was smiling gratefully. "You're quite the knight in shining armor now."

He blushed a fiery red. "Oh, come now, it's not so very wonderful. Rather a lark, really. And besides, I never dreamt I'd ever get the chance to rescue anybody in real life, so I suppose it's I who should be thanking you!"

She laughed. "I don't think you'll be thanking me this time tomorrow, when you'll be trying to manage a Channel crossing with a fidgety three-year-old. I only pray that she's not prone to *mal de mer!*"

"Good God!" The thought brought a look of horror to Wilbur's face, until he caught Amanda's teasing expression.

She then knelt and gave the child a brief hug.

"*Maman, maman,* are you going away?" Celeste cried out.

Amanda shook her head ruefully. "I cannot be your mother, *chérie.* Wilbur here will take you to a man who will love you; he'll be both a *maman* and a *papa* for you. Goodbye." She kissed the little girl's cheek and stood up, blinking away a tear.

"And as for you, Wilbur," she turned towards him, "thank you once more for being such a good friend. This would all have been impossible without your assistance, and I shall never forget you." Raising herself on tiptoe, she planted a warm kiss upon his smooth cheek.

Inspired by a sudden boldness, he returned the favor, and then blushed once more. To cover his confusion, he spoke up in a brusque, businesslike tone. "Well, I'd better be getting my things together, if my little 'niece' and I are going to reach the coast in time."

"Are you certain that you have everything you need?" Amanda inquired anxiously. "The clothes, the money, the address, the—"

"Colonel Josiah Thornton, Maplewood, Surrey," Wilbur recited dutifully. "And yes, I've got plenty of blunt, and no, I shan't forget anything. It will all go smooth as silk, you'll see."

"Of course," she smiled. "And if anything should go wrong," she dived momentarily into the carriage, reappearing with something in her hand, "you can always rely upon this!" They both laughed as she handed him the forgotten bottle of gin.

The coachman emitted a muffled sound, which Amanda interpreted as a token of his impatience; after all, the air was too chilly for the horses to be kept standing. "Have a safe journey," she called, climbing into the carriage, "and I promise I shall be in contact with you soon." She gave them a final wave as they turned to go into the hotel.

On the way home at last, Amanda relaxed and closed her eyes, exhausted despite the fact that it was still before noontime. The morning had been an emotional ordeal, and although the results had been successful, Amanda was thankful for it to be over at last.

The carriage came to a halt in front of Louis's house, and a groom stepped forward to take the horses' heads, as the coachman climbed down from the box. Amanda, who had alighted without assistance, turned to thank him for his services, but before she could speak, he strode towards her and unexpectedly seized her arm in a painful grip. Her startled eyes flew to his, and her heart lurched as she recognized that wrenchingly familiar gaze, even before he tore the scarf from around his face.

"Come with me." Nick virtually dragged her into the house, not pausing until they were in the library, with the door slammed shut behind them. He drew a deep breath, as if to force his anger under control, but his pale eyes still burned as if they could strip flesh from bone.

For a panicked instant, Amanda wondered whether he would actually do her bodily harm. She doubted it, no matter how angry he may be; and besides, she had done nothing wrong! But why then was her heart pounding so violently? She sat down in a nearby chair, to conceal the trembling of her limbs.

He addressed her in a cold, silky voice. "You are by now aware that it was I who drove you about on your little adventure this morning. Now, if it would not be too much trouble, would you be so kind as to tell me what in blazes was going on?"

She had no choice but to tell him the truth, trying in vain to keep her voice from faltering under his intense scrutiny. At times his mouth seemed to twist in what might have been distaste, but at least he did not interrupt her until she had given him a full recital of events, beginning with her very first meeting with the Baron. Amanda refrained only from mentioning exactly where that meeting had taken place.

She was well aware that at various points her story must have sounded farfetched, but to her relief, Nick remained silent, not pressing her for details.

How appealing she is, he thought to himself as she spoke, and how deceitful! Had he not known already that the child was hers, he might even have believed her tale. But even so, it was a useful exercise. He had given her the opportunity to be honest with him, to tell him the truth about this child of a previous liaison, and she had answered him with lies. That told him all he wished to know, but somehow the knowledge made him feel a kind of angry despair.

And how close he had come to the brink of disaster! For despite the air of unconcern which he had so carefully maintained, the past weeks of Amanda's company had undermined many of his defenses. He had found himself too aware of her presence, and had purposely put distance between them; he had felt in himself the desire to be gentle towards her, and had therefore forced himself to be brusque and unsympathetic. But unsuitable though she was, and despite his loathing of emotional ties, the girl had gotten under his skin. Had he not just learned that she was as faithless as any other female, who knows but what he might have weakened to the point of offering his hand and his heart.

"Well, I must say," she concluded at last, glancing up at his impassive face, "if I had known how receptive you would be to all this, I would have told you everything from the beginning. You might even have been a help." She attempted a smile.

He moved away from her, finally removing his heavy greatcoat, and stepping up to a mirror, as if he had forgotten her presence. For the next several minutes he adjusted the folds of his cravat, apparently lost in deep concentration. Then he swung about to face her.

"Very well, then. That's that, I suppose. But tell me one thing, Amanda." The question had been plaguing him for some time now, and he could not prevent himself from asking it. "Was it not difficult for you to send the child away?"

She looked at him in puzzlement. "No, why should it have been? I knew that she'd be vastly better off with Thornton than she would be in that awful hovel. And besides, even though she was a dear creature, whatever would I do with a child here? Surely you're not suggesting that I should have kept her myself!"

Nick could not prevent himself from wincing slightly at this callous rejection of motherhood, but the expression was controlled so swiftly that she failed to perceive it.

"No, I realize it would be impossible," he acknowledged bluntly. "Few men in this world would look at you twice, if you had another man's child in tow. At least not until you had been married at least once."

"Oh, at least!" Amanda echoed, smiling with an amusement which he could not share. "And now, if you are satisfied, Nick, I'd like to go upstairs. I am promised to drive out this afternoon, and I must change my clothes. Please believe me, I am very sorry to have been a worry to you and Louis, but I'm certain you will agree that all was for the best."

As she spoke, she rose gracefully to her feet, and Nick found his eyes drawn to the trim lines of her figure, and the waist which he had spanned with his own hands. No, she did not look as if she had borne a child. Instead she still looked virginal and untouched, with those disarmingly honest eyes.

He cursed his own weakness as she departed, bitterly aware that this new and damning knowledge did nothing to diminish the power of her attraction.

During the next few days, Amanda was able to go about the social rounds with a lighter heart. Her own situation was still unresolved, but whenever she thought of little Celeste, she felt a warm relief; in one small way, her awkward plight had had a favorable result, and she could almost be grateful for the circumstances which had brought her to Paris. Fortune had favored her once, and it was not impossible that it would do so again, when it came time to decide her own fate. For the moment, she was human enough to enjoy the hedonistic pleasure of being well dressed, well lodged, and much courted; heaven only knew if such delights would come her way in future.

She saw little of Nick. He appeared to devote himself to pleasures which kept him out until the early hours each morning. Rarely did he cross Amanda's path, a circumstance for which she was grateful; after all, his presence was too disturbing for her peace of mind. Still, she found herself searching for him in every crowd, and losing the edge of her enthusiasm when she realized he was not there.

It was therefore with some surprise that she walked into the library one evening and found him sprawled in a leather easy chair. A much-depleted decanter of brandy rested upon a nearby table.

"Come here, Amanda. I want to talk to you."

179

Puzzled, she obeyed the peremptory command and moved forward, seating herself in the chair opposite him.

He crossed one slimly booted foot over the other, and surveyed her critically from head to toe. "You've changed," he said abruptly. And it was true: the dowdy country miss was gone forever, replaced by a poised, strikingly attractive lady of fashion. New clothes had revealed the perfection of her figure and the subtle radiance of her coloring; and social experience had given her a more confident bearing. Judging from the grim expression of Nick's face, however, the transformation gave him no pleasure to contemplate.

Amanda endured his scrutiny unflinchingly, until her patience began to wear thin. "Well, do I pass muster?" she inquired drily.

He did not smile. "Yes, you do indeed," he replied, although his tone stripped the statement of any complimentary effect. "In fact, you have played your part so well that now it is time to end the game."

"What on earth do you mean?" she asked, feeling suddenly chilled.

Nick swirled the brandy in his glass, seemingly engrossed in the liquid's golden depths. "I mean that everything has proceeded exactly as I had hoped. Today I received an offer for your hand."

The words should have come as no surprise, but Amanda was nonetheless shocked. "From whom?" she managed to inquire.

"Whom else?" he taunted. "Young De Colombe."

"Oh, no!" She could not repress the whispered exclamation. Of all the gentlemen who paid her court, Philippe was the most vulnerable to hurt, and therefore the one whom she least wished to form a serious attachment.

"Come now," Nick said impatiently, "surely you were expecting it. Thanks to your efforts, he's really quite infatuated. Indeed, he was an ideal choice, my dear: stupid enough to swallow the faradiddle about your lack of dowry, rich enough to keep you in high style, and naive enough to trust you completely. You'll be able to lead him round by the nose—in all, the perfect husband."

"Stop it, Nick!" she cried out, unable to listen to more of these sneering words. "You're being cruel—he's just a boy!"

"Not too young for you to marry him."

"Indeed he is, and I'll do no such thing!"

"Oh?" Nick set his glass down, his jaw set and expression hard. "I think you shall. I'm tired of this charade, and I want it ended. You've disrupted my life more than sufficiently as it is, and I have no mind to wait patiently while you cast about for bigger fish."

"But you don't understand," Amanda protested. "I don't wish to be married at all! And even if I did, the last person I would ever choose would be Philippe. He's too good, too kind a person for such a callous deception."

"Oh my, my, such scruples." Nick's quiet voice was like the lash of a whip. "Has someone more attractive offered you a *carte blanche?* Believe me, it is far better to marry Philippe and then to take your pleasures where you will. And in any case, the matter is decided. I gave him my permission, and he has applied for a special license for your marriage. There will be a private ceremony tomorrow, after which the two of you will retire quietly to his estate in Anjou.''

"You can't be serious," Amanda pleaded desperately. "He has never even breathed a word of this to me!"

"Why should he? I assured him that you were madly in love with him, and that your heart's desire was to be swept off directly to the church."

"You are vile." Amanda struggled to keep her voice steady, though her whole world was rocking upon its foundations. "You don't care whom you hurt, do you? How dare you speak of love and heart's desires, you don't know the meaning of the words! I will not do this thing, Nick, I will *not!*"

"Yes, you will." Her scathing words had brought a slight flush to his cheeks, but his voice remained steady and cold. "Perhaps you've forgotten the offer you received from our friend the Baron; I have not. He's quite an eligible *parti*, you know, and I'm confident that he would provide me with a large financial settlement as a token of his gratitude. If I hand you over to him, you would soon agree to marriage; you see, I have great faith in his powers of persuasion."

Amanda could not repress the shudder of horror which Nick's words evoked. She clenched her fists tightly, silently vowing to resist both of these schemes with her last breath. It would break her heart to deceive dear loyal Philippe—and as for the Baron, she would rather die than have him touch her again. And she had believed that Nick shared her feelings, and would protect her!

But what could she do? The only alternative left to her was to leave the house, and though that prospect was frightening, she at least had some money left over from the sum Nick had given her. That amount had been greatly reduced by her rescue of Celeste, but at least she could manage a few days' bed and board at an inn, until she could determine what to do next. She said none of this aloud, however; if Nick believed in her compliance, he would relax his guard and she would be able to escape from the house during the night.

Summoning all of her self-control, she forced her face to assume an expression of resignation. "Very well, Nick," she said bleakly. "You win. I shall do as you say."

"Good." Despite the curt word, he did not seem pleased; in fact, his harsh expression deepened into a scowl.

"What time will Philippe arrive tomorrow?" she dared to ask.

"At two o'clock."

She rose to her feet. "Then if you will excuse me, I must see to my packing now." She made her way a little shakily to the door, but his voice halted her upon the threshold.

"You'd do better to get some sleep. You'll want to look your best tomorrow for your wedding."

The contemptuous edge in his voice was too

much, and her fragile control snapped. She whirled to face him with angry tears in her eyes. "You may take your helpful advice, Sir Nicholas Malvern, and go straight to blazes!" Her vision blurred, and she fumbled for the latch; somehow, she found it, and a moment later the door closed behind her with a resounding slam.

There was no reason to feel so miserable, Amanda told herself fiercely a few minutes later, as she sat in her room and struggled to master the emotions warring within her. She would leave here and be her own mistress, answerable to no one; in fact, at this very moment she should be packing, or plotting her escape. Why then did the image of Nick's harsh face keep rising before her tear-washed eyes?

He despised her, and now was arranging to be rid of her burdensome presence. By all rights she should hate him in return, but she could not. Instead she was tortured by the thought of never seeing him again. To live without ever hearing his voice or feeling his presence would be an agony.

The door swung open with a sudden crash, and Nick strode into the room. Startled, Amanda leaped to her feet, realizing that she had left the door unbolted in her confusion. Then she hastily turned her back upon him, fumbling in her pocket for a handkerchief as she heard the door slam behind him.

He seized her roughly by the shoulders and swung her around to face him. "I won't let you go like this," he rasped. "I've tried to master it, but I can't." Then for the first time he noticed her tears, and a strange expression came over his face. Releasing her shoulders, he brought his hands up to cup her face, his thumbs brushing lightly against her wet lashes. "You accuse me of not understanding love, of not having a heart." His voice was low, intense. "That was true once—but not since I met you. No matter how hard I tried to ignore you or dislike you, you were always there, so brave and clever, and more beautiful than I dared admit. You've gotten under my skin, damn you."

His eyes held hers with such burning resolve that she could not breathe. "I never thought I would say this to any woman, but I've fallen in love with you. I can't fight it any longer, Amanda. How can I let you go to another man, without ever having taken you for my own?" He buried his face suddenly in the softness of her hair, as his fingers gripped her neck with convulsive strength.

In one, incredible, magical instant, Amanda's heart flooded with a joy such as she had never known. It was as if all her misery had been erased in a single stroke, at the sound of Nick's words. Never for one moment had she imagined that her feelings might be returned, but now the impossible had become real: he loved her!

With sudden insight, she understood his harshness towards her, as an attempt to deny his own feelings. Trembling slightly, she reached to slide her arms around him, feeling the sudden tensing of his powerful shoulders. Could it be that he was unsure of her love? "Nick," she breathed, her voice a soft caress. "I love you, too. I have for the longest time."

He raised his head to scan her features with a swift searching look, and the truth of her words was there for him to read in her glowing eyes and hesitant smile. With a cry almost of exultation, he caught her to him fiercely, lifting her slightly off the ground, as his mouth descended to claim its prize. His lips were almost bruising in their force, but Amanda did not care, as she clung to him with equal fervor.

Gradually he lowered her to the ground, loosening the steely pressure of his arms as he reached to remove the pins from her hair. The soft honey-colored cloud tumbled down her back, and he combed his long fingers through it as if in a daze. "You were well named, my darling," he murmured. "You were made to be loved."

"Only by you," she replied softly. "Only by you." She raised one hand to trace the firm outline of his jaw, in wonder that all this could be quite real, and not a dream. "There could be no greater joy for me in all the world than to be loved by you, and to be your wife."

Abruptly his free hand seized hers, stilling its movement. "Amanda, let us not pretend to misunderstand each other." Nick's tone had suddenly lost its gentleness. "You know quite well that I cannot marry you."

There was a peculiar buzzing in Amanda's ears, and if it had not been for Nick's arm supporting her waist, she might have swayed a little. "No, I'm afraid I don't. I don't know that at all." It seemed to her that her voice was coming from a great distance. "You said that you loved me, Nick."

He moved both hands to grip her shoulders, effectively creating a space between them. "Yes, by God, I do, but I have obligations which cannot be ignored."

Amanda forced herself to meet his eyes, but the mixture of regret and impatience which she read there was almost more than she could bear.

"I am a Malvern," he continued, with that familiar touch of arrogance she had so despised, "and I have a duty to that name. You must see that marriage to someone in your position would be utterly out of the question. I need a wife who comes to me with her reputation untarnished, not one unfit to be received even by her own family!"

His cruel words sliced into her, until she thought she must cry out from the pain. But no word or sound could force its way past the tight ache in her throat, and she stood motionless and pale, her eyes closed, waiting for the next blow.

She could hear the frown in Nick's voice as he spoke again. "Damn it all, Amanda, this is not the way I might have wished for things to turn out. But at least we'll have this one night together, before you marry De Colombe in the morning."

Amanda opened her eyes at that, although she did not look up at him. Was this nightmare truly happening, or was there some way of changing Nick's mind? "I will not marry Philippe," she said, though her words came out as a mere whisper. "I love you, Nick; I could never marry another man." There, it was done now. She'd lowered her pride as far as it could go.

"Darling—" Nick gave her an exasperated little shake. "This opportunity with De Colombe is one which won't come your way again! The boy will never know how many lovers you've had, and living in France will give you the freedom and respectability you could never enjoy in England. You'll thank me for it!"

With a sudden movement Amanda tore free of his grasp, stumbling backwards a few steps. His touch was too painful to be endured now, and she knew that betraying tears would not be long in falling. Anger would serve as a temporary shield, however, and she summoned the last scraps of her dignity.

"I'll thank you only to leave this room," she flung at him, dragging open the door with an eloquent gesture. "No, don't touch me!" she added hastily as Nick moved nearer, and the rising note of near-hysteria in her voice stopped him in his tracks.

"You've no cause to upset yourself like this, Amanda," he said after a brief pause. "You'll see that I'm right in the end. Just let me love you tonight, and—"

"Get *out!*" she interrupted, and when Nick's concerned glance took in her feverishly glittering eyes and rigid posture, he frowned.

"We'll speak again in the morning, darling," he said, a shade too calmly. "Things will look different after a night's sleep." He walked to the door, pausing at the threshold. "You and I have not yet finished with each other, Amanda." He reached out a hand and lightly touched her lips before she could flinch away. Then he was gone, and Amanda barely had time to slam the door and turn the key before the first silent sob caught at her throat.

Chapter Nine

How long she had been weeping, she could not tell. All she knew was that her body felt racked and drained, as though her life spirit had ebbed away with her tears.

With a weak hand, Amanda brushed the hair back from her eyes. She forced herself to sit up, swinging her legs over the edge of the bed. There was no more time to be lost; the light of early morning shone behind the drawn curtains. If she were going to escape this nightmare, it would have to be before Philippe arrived.

Moving slowly, like an old woman, she went to the wardrobe and pulled out a heavy cloak and a small satchel to carry a few essentials. At the very back, she saw the old dress in which she had first arrived, and without even stopping to consider, she pulled it out and changed into it. Everything else had been brought by Nick, and she would not be beholden to him for more than was absolutely necessary. Indeed, after the cruel way in which he had used her, manipulating her deepest emotions, she did not want to think of him ever again; but even that angry resolve brought a fresh wave of pain.

Even worse was the way in which she had humiliated herself, confessing her love even after he had made it clear that his plans for her were unchanged. How could she have lost all sense of pride and self-respect? No matter what he thought of her, she was still Amanda Waverley.

But in other ways, she was not at all the same. In the last twelve hours, she had been catapulted from a state of acute misery to a fool's paradise, swept away by a love which had blinded her natural judgment and sense of caution. And then her dream world had been shattered, leaving only a despair which was all the more excruciating for the rapturous emotion which had gone before. Amanda felt as battered as if she had been physically beaten, and in the aftermath, a blessed numbness enveloped her senses. It was a fragile defense, but perhaps it would last long enough to get her past the next few hours.

Amanda wrapped herself in her cloak, picked up the satchel, and made her way downstairs. There were no servants in sight, and the library door was firmly shut, hinting at Nick's presence within. It took only a moment to step into the foyer, silently slide back the bolt on the front door, and escape to the street.

Once outside, she began to walk blindly, little caring where she went. All that mattered was to get away. Then suddenly she heard her name being called, and as she turned around, her heart leaped for a delirious instant. Was it—?

It was Louis. "*Chérie*, where are you going, alone and in those abominable clothes?" He approached her, clad in riding dress and still holding a whip in his hand. "I was just going out to— But wait, something is the matter!"

The concern in his voice almost broke through her fragile reserve. She could not tell him the truth, but it seemed only right to say goodbye. Looking up at him, she was unaware of how much her red-rimmed eyes and white face betrayed.

"Louis, I am going away," she said quietly. "Nick and I have a terrible row, and I have no choice but to leave him."

Louis's dark eyes widened in surprise. Tucking his riding whip under his arm, he reached to take both of her hands in his. "You wish to run away? But surely this thing can be discussed. I have confidence that Nick—"

"No, no!" Amanda broke in. "Please believe me, it is too late for that. There is no other solution, Louis." She attempted a smile. "I felt that as a friend I owed you an explanation, but I am not asking you to be disloyal to Nick. Don't worry about me, I shall be well enough, but I would be grateful if you would not tell Nick that you have seen me."

She reached up and brushed a kiss across his cheek, but when she would have turned away, he clung to her hands in a relentless grip.

"Amanda, you must let me help you," he exclaimed. "I do not know what this trouble is between you and Nick, but for a young girl to be alone in Paris—*Mordieu*, it is not to be thought of! If you must run away, let me take you to my hunting box. It is in the countryside, near Chantilly, and very remote. No one will see you there, and when things are resolved, you can easily return and—"

"Oh, Louis, no!" Amanda's voice was tinged with desperation. "Don't you see? Things will not be resolved, and I cannot go back to him, Louis, I—"

"Then we shall go to Chantilly, and I shall not trouble you with any more questions. Come along!" Louis was suddenly brisk and efficient, as if he realized that she was near to breaking point. Gently he steered her towards the stables, and within a few minutes, his fastest horse had been hitched between the shafts of the phaeton. Louis handed her up, and then with a flick of the reins, they clattered off in the direction of the city gates.

It took them a long while to reach Chantilly, and by the time they arrived Amanda was completely exhausted, as much by her emotional state as by the journey itself. Images of Nick kept surfacing in her mind, despite her conscious determination not to think of him. He would have discovered her absence by now, and she wondered what excuse he would make to Philippe. She hoped that the interview would be acutely embarrassing for him; it was the least he deserved. As for herself, she knew she ought to be deciding what to do, but she could not, not while her mind and body felt drugged, refusing to function. When they finally arrived at the house, Louis had to lift her from the seat and carry her inside.

Tenderly he laid her upon a sofa which was still draped with its holland cover, and then he set about pulling back the dusty curtains. The afternoon sun fell warmly upon her face, and Amanda drifted almost immediately into sleep.

When she awoke some hours later, the room was in shadow. She sat up, feeling dizzy and not much refreshed, and saw that a note from Louis was propped upon a nearby table.

"My dear Amanda," it read, "I have not the heart to derange you, but I must leave now. I will send a girl from the village to attend you, and bring you food. Tomorrow I shall return, and we will talk. Until then, I say nothing to Nick. Do not worry. I embrace you, Louis."

Shortly afterwards, a tentative knock sounded upon the door, and a young girl entered the room, executing a clumsy curtsey. "Would Madame want to eat something? It is already past five o'clock!" she said in French, with a slurred country accent.

In spite of her misery Amanda smiled, thanking the girl for her trouble. Food was the last thing she wanted now, but there was no escaping the fact that she must eat to live, and live she must. Without him.

That thought was in Amanda's mind again as she stood once more upon the deck of the Channel packet, this time watching the French coastline disappear into the haze. It was warmer and less windy than it had been before, but there was a chill which emanated from within her, from the place where she had recently felt so happy and alive.

Louis had been more than wonderful. It was he who had helped to put the world back upon its axis, by offering gentle sympathy without probing further into what had happened between her and Nick. Inventing an explanation for *Tante* Sophie, who in any case never fatigued herself with the comings and goings of her guests, he had returned to Chantilly and spent long hours with Amanda, trying to coax her out of her depression. At last she had smiled to please him, unable to stand seeing him infected by her own misery.

He had also evinced great horror at her expressed desire to seek employment, and had flatly refused to offer her any assistance in that direction. Instead, he had insisted that there must be someone in England who knew her, and who would be willing to offer her a refuge. Amanda could not confide the truth without revealing all the lies which she had told before, and so she answered his questions evasively. Before long, however, his probing awakened a long-forgotten memory. There was indeed one neighbor who had known Amanda, and who had cared little for her stepmother's power. It was Squire Barnett, Peter's father.

She had not seen him for years, and after her disgrace, Amanda had never received any reply to her letters. Now she scarcely even knew whether he was still alive. She rather thought that he was, because rumours of his death would have reached her through the servants. It was uncertain, however, as to how he would react to seeing her again.

In any case, Louis was intent upon sending her back to England, confident that her fears were simply the exaggerations of an adolescent. In her apathetic state of mind, it seemed that she may as well try this one possible avenue of help; if it proved to be unsuccessful, and she were unable to find even the most menial post somewhere, there would always be another way out of her difficulties. And if it were to be so, it would be far better for her to be in England, with Louis secure in the belief that she was well and happy.

As for Nick, he had made it clear enough that he wished to have no part in her life. Had he really said that he loved her? It seemed so long ago now, as if it had happened in a dream. She had believed him; but perhaps that was because she wanted so much to believe.

From the moment of their meeting, he had treated her with indifference and occasionally even contempt. How could she have been so foolish as to think that what he called love bore any resemblance to her own tender trusting feelings? Because of her own folly, he had hurt her worse than she had ever imagined possible, and it was only that blessed numbness which kept her going through the empty days.

Louis had seen her off on the mail coach with cheerful relief, having persuaded her to accept a large purse holding more than enough to cover her expenses for the journey. As she hugged him good-bye, however, Amanda had to choke back a sob;

despite their brief acquaintance, he had offered the kind of selfless friendship which had been all too rare in her experience.

Now, as she watched the coastline slowly fade from sight, she could not help thinking what a changed person she was from the impulsive idealistic girl who had left those shores only a few weeks previously. Then she had been full of hope and expectation, but now that spirit had been drained from her. No one had approached her this time, even though she was obviously alone; there was an aura of frozen reserve about her, discouraging even the most brash of her fellow travellers.

After another long uncomfortable day of travel, it was dusk when the coach finally stopped at the town of Staplehurst, where Amanda descended with her small portmanteau. A moment later the street was deserted, and she set off briskly in the direction of Barnett Manor, before she could be seen by any curious passersby.

The distance was roughly four miles, and darkness had fallen by the time she arrived at the manor. As she approached up the winding drive, she could see light through the tall windows, indicating at least that someone was in residence. Amanda thought of the many times she had taken this same path in happier days; now she could only hope that it led to sanctuary, and not despair.

The heavy brass knocker fell with a resounding thud. After a minute or two during which there was no response, Amanda sounded it again. She stood waiting, frozen with discouragement, and then as she was about to turn away, there was the scraping sound of heavy bolts being pulled back. Slowly the door creaked open, and Amanda found herself face to face with an old man, who blinked at her with watery shortsighted eyes.

"Yes, miss?" he said impatiently. "What do you want?"

Amanda smiled, a little sadly. "Padgett, don't you remember me?"

At the sound of her voice, the old man started, then peered at her more closely. "Is that you, Miss Amanda?" he murmured in disbelief.

"Yes, it is," she answered gently. "I've come back, and I'm sorry that it's been such a long time."

Almost without conscious thought, she moved forward to plant a kiss upon the old man's lined cheek, and for a moment he clutched at her; then he remembered his position, and drew back stiffly. When he spoke again, however, his voice was slightly hoarse.

"It's a pleasure to see you again, Miss Amanda. The master has missed you a good deal."

She hid her smile at the formality with which Padgett had always concealed his own feelings. "I've missed him as well. May I see him now?"

Padgett seemed taken aback, as if suddenly recalling the lateness of the hour and the oddness of Amanda's arrival, alone upon the doorstep, but he stepped backward and motioned for her to come in. She did so, setting down her bag in the hallway.

"If you'll just wait a moment, Miss Amanda, I'll tell him that you are here." So saying, he disappeared behind the great doors of the library.

Amanda looked around her, seeing the mirrors and paintings, the foyer and staircase which were as familiar to her as if she had seen them only yesterday. It was strange to think that almost six years had passed since she had stood here, listening to the echo of Peter's cheerful voice.

"So you've finally decided to pay a visit, have you?" A gruff voice which she knew well startled her out of her reverie, and she spun around to see Squire Barnett standing in the hall. He seemed to have shrunk slightly, his clothes hanging more loosely upon his large frame, and he leaned upon a knotted wood cane, but his eyes still burned a bright blue. He did not smile as he watched her. "Why have you come?"

Amanda met his gaze composedly. Once she would have been flustered by his abrupt manner, but now she was wiser, recognizing that his rudeness concealed deeper feelings.

"I have come to ask for your help," she stated quietly.

He frowned at her. "Why me? Where's that busybody stepmother of yours?"

"She has barred me from her house."

There was a moment of shocked silence, and then the Squire shrugged and turned his back upon her, limping slowly back into the library. "Come in and close the door," he ordered, and she silently complied.

Once he had settled himself into an imposing leather armchair, angled to receive the warmth of the crackling fire, he looked up at her from beneath his heavy scowling brows.

"Why did you never visit before?" he barked.

The question was unexpected, and Amanda took a moment before replying. "May I sit down?" she inquired, and when the Squire nodded she seated herself gracefully in a chair facing him.

"There were many times when I wanted to come," she began earnestly, "but after I returned from London, my stepmother forbade me to see you, or indeed any of our neighbors and friends. At first I tried to slip out of the house, but I was too closely watched. Then I tried to write you letters, but when I never received any reply, I assumed that you did not wish to see me."

The Squire's broad fist pounded angrily upon the arm of his chair. "There were no letters! I never saw a one of 'em!"

Amanda's eyes widened in distress. "Then she must have intercepted them. You must have thought that I was avoiding you." Impulsively she moved out of her chair and sank down upon her knees before him, taking his hand between hers. "Please believe me, sir, when I say I am truly sorry for that."

His hand gripped hers in response, but his eyes were still wary. "Why did she do this to you? I know the two of you never got on together, but all this is mighty hard to swallow."

"She despised me for failing to come up to scratch during my season. I refused all my offers, because I was waiting for Peter." Her golden eyes shone briefly with pain. "She did not want that match, and she never forgave me for throwing away my prospects. Don't you remember?"

"Yes, I remember." The Squire's eyes were misted with tears as he remembered his son, and how he had been so much in love with Amanda, and she with him. Foolishly the Squire had thought to make them wait, thinking them too young to form a serious attachment. In so doing he had not only lost his son, but he had fulfilled the spiteful wishes of Lady Ruth. The marriage which she dreaded had indeed never taken place. But clearly Lady Ruth had underestimated the will of her stepdaughter, for if Amanda could not have Peter, she would accept no one. No wonder that her stepmother had sought to punish her.

The Squire patted Amanda's hand with awkward affection. "Don't put yourself in a taking, girl. I always knew it wasn't your fault. Now, you'd better get on with your story, and tell me why that woman's dared to throw you out of your own home."

This would be far more difficult to explain, and Amanda wavered briefly between telling the truth and creating more of the falsehoods which came so easily to her now. But reading the honest old face before her, she knew she could not lie to him.

The thought struck her suddenly that this moment was much like the night in Nick's cottage, when she had unburdened her heart. Then, as well as now, she had felt a mysterious bond of trust with her listener. The familiar ache in her heart surged once more as she acknowledged that with Nick, appearances had been cruelly deceiving.

"Several weeks ago," she commenced bravely, "I was escorting Chloe back from the dressmaker in town, where her fittings had run on into the early evening. The coach was a few miles from home, when we were held up by highwaymen."

The Squire gave an audible cough of surprise, but she merely continued. "Since we had no money or jewels worth the taking, the leader decided to hold me for ransom. He left a note in the coach, and took me . . . somewhere . . . to wait. A letter did arrive a few hours later, but instead of paying the sum, my stepmother refused. She claimed that I had brought disgrace upon myself, and she forbade me ever to return home."

"Infamous!" the Squire expostulated angrily. "That woman should be whipped at the cart's tail—but what happened then? This highwayman—did he harm you?"

"No, he did not," she reassured him. "He behaved quite honorably towards me, I believe." She ignored the Squire's derisive snort. "He turned out to be a gentleman, but wild to a fault, who had held up the coach as a sort of lark. When he realized how much damage he had caused, he decided to keep me with him, and take care of me until I could find a friend to help, or some suitable employment."

At the look upon the Squire's face, she shook her head ruefully. "Despite what you may be thinking, he did not offer me a *carte blanche*. He took me with him to Paris, where we stayed in the house

203

of his aunt and cousin, and he introduced me to society as his sister. He even purchased clothes for me, so that I would not be ashamed." Or rather, so that *he* would not be ashamed, she amended privately. "Then, he hit upon the notion that instead of seeking work, I should try to find myself a husband."

"First sensible notion I've heard so far!" interjected the Squire. "Stands to reason that if your family disowns you, you wouldn't find a husband in the ordinary way. Why didn't you?"

Amanda shook her head. "I did not want a marriage founded upon lies. And besides, I—I had no wish to marry." The Squire peered closely at her heightened color and drew a sudden conclusion.

"Tell me," he commanded, "did you fall in love with that scoundrel?"

Her startled glance flew to his, then dropped to her lap. She did not answer, but her silence was all the confirmation he needed.

"Come to think of it," he went on, "why didn't the rascal just marry you himself?"

"He did not want to be married—least of all to me." Her voice came out almost in a whisper, and she realized that despite her efforts at self-control, she might break down if she told the Squire any more about her relations with Nick. She cleared her throat before continuing. "I almost did marry someone, but he was only an innocent boy, and I found I could not go through with it. So I had to leave, and fortunately I had a friend who lent me the money to come back to England. And at last I thought of you."

She took a deep breath. "I realize that after hearing this, you have every right to be shocked and disgusted; I feel bitterly ashamed of what has happened to me. I am in need of a place to stay temporarily, but if you feel unable to offer one, I shall certainly understand."

There was a pregnant silence until the Squire finally spoke. "This so-called gentleman of yours— before I answer, I want to know his name!"

Amanda raised her golden eyes to the Squire's bright blue ones. "Then you will help me only if I give you that information?" she asked softly.

"Yes!"

She rose determinedly to her feet, her face pale but composed. "Then I will wish you good-night, Squire, and take my leave."

"Oh, for God's sake, girl, sit down!" The Squire waved his hand impatiently. "I'd forgotten what an impertinent miss you were! Now get down off those high ropes of yours and pour me a glass of sherry. Pour yourself one, too. And ring the bell for Padgett, so he can set another place for supper."

The effects of Amanda's disappearance were not immediately apparent. When Louis strolled into his parlor that first evening, he had found Nick pacing back and forth in front of the fireplace, and at Louis's entrance he looked up sharply.

"Have you seen her?" he demanded.

"Seen who, my friend?" Louis inquired blandly, settling himself in a comfortable chair.

"Amanda. She's not in the house."

"Is that so remarkable? Perhaps she left to do some shopping, or to pay a visit."

"No, that's impossible. She had an important engagement today—she would not have forgotten it."

Louis sighed. "With a woman, shopping is never impossible. Relax yourself, Nick, she shall return." Then, as he pulled off his gloves, he spoke slowly and deliberately. "Or is there perhaps some reason why you fear she may have gone off, as we say, gallivanting somewhere?"

"No, of course not!" Nick's vehemence was undermined by the faint color which rose to his face. "I'm simply concerned that she might have had some sort of accident. That's all."

"Your affection is touching." Louis rose languidly to his feet. "Now if you will excuse me, I am engaged to dine with Madame Rouget." With a casual wave of his hand, he left the room.

For the next two days, Louis continued to avoid contact with Nick, deliberately waiting for some revelation of Nick's own feelings before Louis would consider betraying Amanda's confidence. No matter what the reason for their dispute, Amanda had clearly been wounded deeply, and not even Louis could forgive Nick for the stricken look upon his sister's face. His liaison with the pretty widow served as a convenient excuse, and he was able to absent himself most of the time, observing in passing that Nick was becoming progressively more haggard-looking. Finally, on the third day, Louis had hoped to creep into the house unnoticed, but his luck was out. No sooner had the front door closed behind him than Nick appeared in the hallway. It was obvious that he had not slept or changed clothes since the previous evening, and his face was etched with grim worry.

He motioned Louis into the library, out of the hearing of the servants, and then threw himself into the chair where he had spent an uncomfortable night.

"Louis, she still hasn't come home. It's been over two days." Nick's voice was cold and matter-of-fact, but his hands were clenched upon the arms of his chair.

"Mon Dieu!" Louis exclaimed feebly, seating himself a few feet away and watching Nick's face closely.

"I thought at first that she was simply angry at not getting her own way, and I was certain that after a night at an inn somewhere, she'd see reason and come back. But now I scarcely know what to think."

"How could this be?" Louis asked curiously. "What happened between you?"

"I wanted her to marry Philippe de Colombe," Nick replied, "and she . . . refused."

"But surely that is not enough for her to run away!"

"You don't know the things I said to her. Unforgivable things." Wearily he leaned his forehead against his right palm. "I drove her out, Louis, and when I think of what could be happening to her, all alone with no money or assistance, by God, I—"

"I beg you, do not distress yourself so," Louis exclaimed reassuringly, moved by his friend's anguish. "I am sure that she has come to no harm. I shall make inquiries, and I promise you that—"

Nick leaped suddenly to his feet, and the look on his face made the words die on Louis's lips. "How is it that you are so sure, my friend?" His green eyes bored into Louis's dark ones with hostile intensity, while his voice was softly menacing. "Do you perhaps know where she is?"

"No, no, you are ridiculous!" Louis's words sounded unconvincing even to his own ears, as he stepped back involuntarily.

With sudden violence, Nick's hands shot out to seize Louis's cravat, almost lifting the smaller man into the air. "Where did you take her? And what was the price—is she now your mistress?"

The blood pounded in Louis's ears as he struggled to shake his head. The fierce grip was loosened, and Louis swayed for a moment, gasping for breath. Then he fixed his eyes accusingly upon Nick's glowering face.

"I do not call you out, Nicholas, because you are so upset, I think you are outside of yourself. But do not do that again!" He found his way to a chair. "Or perhaps I should kill you for Amanda's sake. *Pardieu*, after what you have just admitted, to accuse her again!"

The fiery light died out of Nick's eyes. "Good God, I'm sorry, Louis. You're right, of course. But

I'm half out of my mind with worry—I have got to find her."

"Very well, you shall. Yes, indeed I have her." He checked Nick's angry movement with an upraised hand. "But it is not what you may think. I met her in the street three days ago, just as she was leaving the house; she said that you had argued, and that she needed a place to stay, to hide from you, I think."

Nick winced slightly.

"So I sent her back to England. She said that she would go to a neighbor, an old man named Square or something like. I felt sure that you must know him. But let me tell you, Nick, you must abandon this idea of marrying her to De Colombe, or to anyone she does not wish. Your sister, she is a very unhappy young lady."

Nick uttered a mirthless laugh. "She's not my sister."

Louis started violently. "She is not— But then who—?"

"She is a young lady of quality, who became involved in an ugly situation, very much against her will. Don't ask me questions now, Louis, I haven't time to answer them; I've got a long journey ahead of me, and I can only hope to God I'm not already too late."

"But Nick, wait—what about the man you killed? Is it not still dangerous for you to return to your country?"

Nick shook his head. "I have been making inquiries, and as long as I stay out of London for a while longer, my neck is not at risk. It seems that once the wine mists cleared, a few of the witnesses changed their tune, and were willing to testify that I had responded to an honorable challenge."

He stood up resolutely. "But none of that matters now. I have to find Amanda, and somehow make things right between us. I don't know how I shall do it, but I must; if I don't succeed, I know that I will have wasted the most precious opportunity of my life."

Chapter Ten

The early afternoon sun was casting a soft glow over the Surrey hills as Nick pressed his horse on to a final, weary effort. He had been travelling for more than two days straight, catching only a few hours' exhausted sleep during the Channel crossing, and now his fatigue was giving way to a sense of desperate urgency.

In the course of many hours he had spent pondering Louis's garbled message, he had finally recalled Amanda's saying that her youthful sweetheart had been the son of the local Squire. He had therefore retraced his path to where the fateful abduction had first taken place, and then had asked a farmer to point him towards the Squire's estate. Luckily Nick's memory had served him well, for the man gave him immediate directions to the Barnett manor.

After an hour, however, Nick realized with exasperation that the instructions left much to be desired. He had almost given up hope of finding the place when suddenly it loomed before him, a weathered sprawling house, half-hidden by ancient pines. He found himself thinking of his own estates, much neglected in recent years; the great house would need to be set in order once again, by someone with good taste and determination. Someone very like Amanda . . . His mouth hardened into a grim line as he knocked heavily upon the old oaken door.

A few minutes later, he was ushered by a dour-faced old fossil into a dusty library, only to confront yet another old relic. This one, however, had startlingly blue eyes which brimmed with disapproval.

"State your business, young man," the Squire commanded irritably. "I haven't got all day to waste." He cast his eyes over his visitor in a frankly appraising stare; he saw a tall pale young man of obvious means, whose well-tailored clothes were disarrayed from hard riding, and whose handsome face was marred by lines of fatigue and cynicism. It did not take much to guess who this young man must be, but the Squire's face remained impassive as he waited for his guest to speak.

Nick regarded the Squire with a hint of challenge in his intent gaze. "My name is Sir Nicholas Malvern. Forgive me for intruding upon you, Squire, but my business will not take long. I simply wish to know whether Miss Amanda Waverley is currently residing here."

At the mention of Amanda's name, the Squire's eyes narrowed sharply, and he cast Nick another long assessing glance.

"And why might you be wishing to know that, Sir Nicholas?"

"We have private matters to discuss," Nick answered coldly.

"Is that so?" The Squire lowered himself stiffly into his favorite armchair, but without offering a seat to his visitor. "And why do you suppose I might know this young lady?"

"Don't play games with me, sir!" Nick's badly strained temper suddenly snapped. "If she's here, you may as well know that I intend to take her back with me, regardless of what you may say or do!"

"No, you won't, by God," the Squire bellowed, his own ire aroused. "Not until you tell me why you want her, and what you intend to do with her!"

"That is none of your affair, Squire," Nick said bluntly.

"Isn't it? That girl was like a daughter to me, and I won't stand by to see her dragged off to the harem of some young Turk!"

An involuntary smile tugged at the corners of Nick's mouth. "I assure you, sir, I am no Turk."

"Well, if this ain't Turkish treatment you're offering the girl, I'd like to know what it is! Are you going to marry her?"

Nick was momentarily silenced by the Squire's abrupt question. Was he indeed? In the long empty hours since Amanda had vanished, he had come to know that no matter how his reason may protest, he still loved her to the point of obsession. He had embarked upon this mad chase after realizing that he would never know peace until she was

213

once more by his side. But at no time had marriage figured in his plans.

"Don't think she's good enough for you, eh?" the Squire's impatient voice broke into his thoughts. "Well, that girl has more fine qualities than any woman ever born, and you're a damned fool not to see it!"

"You're quite mistaken," Nick contradicted. "I do see it. If you must know, I happen to love her."

"Ay, that's all well and good, but do you love her enough to offer her more than a *carte blanche?*" The Squire's hands gripped the arms of his chair until the knuckles showed white. "She was going to marry my son, and he was worth ten of you!"

The reference to Peter only reminded Nick of his lingering doubts. "You cannot know the whole circumstances, sir, and I beg you not to interfere in what does not concern you."

"Oho, so that's it!" The Squire met Nick's pale eyes with a look of blazing scorn. "Do you think I don't know that those two passed a night together?"

For once Nick was genuinely startled, and he stared blankly at the older man, who continued to speak.

"I'm no fool, and I knew that anything might have happened when Peter didn't come home until the small hours of that night. But I never thought any the less of Amanda for what she may or may not have done, because I knew she loved my boy with a true heart.

"If you'd lived as long as I have, you young jackanapes, you'd know that many a marriage made for love is consummated long before the vows are spoken. Always have been, always will be—that's human nature. And for all that it's wrong, that don't make a woman into a trollop."

"I know that, damn it," Nick ground out. "I'll admit I was a harsh judge at first, but as I got to know her better, I was ready to give her the benefit of all doubt. Lord knows I've never heeded the proprieties much myself. But that wasn't all, Squire." He squared his shoulders and took a deep breath, aware that there was no gentle way to break such news to the old man. "I have reason to believe that she bore an illegitimate child, whom she sent to France and left to be raised in the most appalling conditions of neglect."

The Squire blanched. "Whose child—Peter's?"

"No, no!" Nick hastened to lay that cruel notion to rest. "It was someone else, a man named Colonel Josiah Thornton."

The Squire's cheeks slowly turned from an ashen hue to a rosy red, while his blue eyes seemed to start from his head. Then he erupted into a loud gust of laughter which made Nick start in surprise.

"Josiah—ha, ha!—Josiah Thornton! Ha! Ha! Lord bless us! Ha, ha!" The Squire wiped his eyes, wheezing, as Nick watched him in growing concern and bewilderment. "Listen to me, my boy, my old friend Colonel Josiah Thornton must be seventy-five years old if he's a day!"

Nick tensed with shock. Seventy-five—?

"Don't know where you could have gotten such a crack-brained tale," the Squire continued. "Besides, I think his daughter and Amanda were school friends. And Josiah ain't the man to be giving a slip on the shoulder to his daughter's classmates—though he might wish he could nowadays!" The Squire settled back in his armchair, still chuckling. "Now tell me, Sir Nicholas, what's all this about a child?"

Nick slowly shook his head, speaking almost to himself. "Amanda told me a tale. She said that a friend of hers had died, leaving the child to a husband who was the worst kind of wastrel. She said that she was sending the child to England, to be with her friend's father."

"Well?" the Squire demanded.

"I didn't believe her." Nick's voice was very quiet. "I had heard the child call her Mama."

"You didn't believe her?" All amusement suddenly vanished from the Squire's face. "What's the matter with you, boy! You say you love this girl, but it seems you're mighty anxious to think the worst of her. With all your mistrust and suspicions, Sir Nicholas, it's no wonder she ran away from you!"

Nick's face looked suddenly drawn. It all seemed so simple now; why could he not have trusted Amanda from the very beginning? It dawned upon him that she had always been truthful with him, up until that very last moment of complete vulnerability, when she had laid open her heart and he had virtually ground it under his heel. She had

216

loved him enough to give him the gift of herself, and in exchange he had offered her only cruelty and insult.

He moved to the window and stared out at the expanse of lawn with unseeing eyes. "You need say no more, sir," he said, and his voice was tinged with self-contempt. "I know now what a bloody idiot I've been, and I know also that it's too late to make amends. I think she loved me once, but I've done everything possible to turn that love to hate."

The Squire leaned forward, watching the young man closely. "She still loves you, boy."

Nick's head turned sharply, his pale eyes boring intently into the Squire's face.

"I saw that look in her eyes before, when my son was alive . . ." the Squire paused to clear his throat. "And I see it again now. But I also see that she's been hurt, and badly so. It'll be her trust that you'll have to regain, if you still want her."

"I do." Nick's words rang with solemn promise. "Will you tell me where she is?"

The two men regarded each other in a brief contest of wills, until the Squire was satisfied with what he read in Nick's steadfast gaze.

"She's out on the lower terrace. But in my day, young men showed a little more respect for their elders when they took their leave!" he added sharply as Nick bolted for the door.

Nick paused upon the threshold and executed a small ironic bow in the Squire's direction. "Forgive me, sir. Indeed I am most grateful for your kind assistance." His words were accompanied by a humorous smile, so charming that the Squire's last doubt was erased. This Sir Nicholas was a devil, the Squire thought, but he'd know how to make a woman happy.

Stepping out through the wide French doors, Nick paused as he perceived an ornamental garden, ringed by tall shrubs. Neglected in this season, it had gone to weeds, but he could discern a pathway skirting the garden's edge. He headed towards it with impatient strides.

As the path rounded a corner, he saw her. Amanda sat facing away from him on a carved wooden bench, with an open book resting in her lap. But she was not reading; her head was turned away, toward where the garden opened out onto the desolate lawns. Nick stopped in his tracks, feeling the fire of his impatience fade into an unaccustomed hesitancy; she looked so vulnerable, with the delicate column of her neck tilted as if weighed down by fatigue or sorrow.

"Amanda." Not wishing to startle her, he called her name in a quiet caressing voice.

Her head jerked up, and she leaped to her feet as if pulled by strings, whirling to face him. Instinctively she clutched the book to her breast as though it might protect her; her golden eyes were wide but somehow wary, and he could see the shadows underneath them.

It was a terrific shock to see him again so unexpectedly, especially when he had been the object of her thoughts a moment beforehand. It was almost as though her tormented brain had actually conjured up his image. And here he was, before her eyes, as arrogantly handsome and magnetic as ever.

She spoke the first question that sprang into her mind, hoping that he could not hear the frantic pounding of her heart. "How did you know I was here?"

"Quite simple," he replied evenly. "I have a good memory, and when Louis mentioned the Squire, I knew where you would be."

"Louis told you?" Amanda felt dismay tear at her. "He promised me . . ."

"Don't blame him. He had no intention of revealing your plans, but I, er," Nick paused, and his mouth curled upwards in memory, "persuaded him."

Amanda fought the hurt in the only way she could, by stirring up the banked coals of her anger. "I might have expected that you'd coerce him," she said icily. "You'll go to any lengths to manipulate people, won't you? You've even followed me all this way, because I wouldn't fall in with your despicable schemes. Well, you can just turn around and go back, because I have had enough of being your pawn!"

"You don't understand, Amanda." Nick shook his head, ruefully aware that this would be every bit as difficult as he had feared. "I need to have you back with me." He took a step closer toward her, but she quickly retreated behind the bench.

"Did you? How very flattering!" Her voice was laced with bitter irony. "And I thought you were so anxious to be rid of me. What happened? Did poor Philippe manage to wring your heart, or did the Baron offer you a few extra thousand?"

Nick's brows drew together as he struggled to ignore her taunt. "I came for myself alone, Amanda. God knows you have every right to be angry, but if you will just listen to me, I—"

"Listen to you? I've done enough of that, thank you—enough for a lifetime!" She choked a little, and cleared her throat. "There's nothing left to discuss!"

He took a deep breath and began again. "We've both made mistakes, love, but—"

"How *dare* you use that word with me!" she broke in angrily. "Have you forgotten what kind of woman I am? You'd better go away and leave me alone, before you become further sullied by my presence!"

Nick ground his teeth in exasperation, and threw caution to the winds. In one swift movement he was over the bench; snaking one arm around her waist, he pulled her tightly against him, ignoring her frantic struggles, while his other hand clamped down over her mouth.

"Will you be quiet, damn it!" he hissed. "You're going to listen to me whether you like it or not. I'm deeply sorry for the things I said to you. I was wrong. I do love you, Amanda, and I can't live without you."

She blinked as the words were fired rapidly at her, and abruptly her struggles ceased.

"These last few days have been torture," he continued more quietly, easing the pressure of his restraining hold but not yet releasing her. "I don't know why I was so cruel, Amanda. Perhaps I wanted to hurt you because you made me feel ashamed of myself. All I know now is that I need you; I need your goodness, your warmth, and if it's not too late, your love. I came here to ask—no, to *beg* you to come back with me."

His voice shook slightly at the final words, and Amanda read the deep emotion in his eyes as her own swam with sudden tears. Then gently he lifted his hand from her mouth, replacing it with his lips.

She shuddered for an instant, and then without conscious volition she was returning his kiss with all the passion pent up in her bruised heart. Her hands clung convulsively to his shoulders, as he held her in a crushing embrace.

There was no use fighting it any more. Over the last few days, Amanda had tried to harden her heart against the memory of him, and against her inner pain. But now, all it took was one look, one touch, and she was once more at his command. If he wanted her, on any terms, she had no strength to refuse him. It did not seem to matter any more that being his mistress meant abandoning her honor and self-respect, and suffering the pain of knowing that his love was not as great as hers. She would give herself to him, until the inevitable time when he wanted her no longer.

He released her mouth and pulled back, watching her face. "Your kiss tells me how you feel, sweetheart, but I need to hear it from your beautiful lips."

She could feel the tautness of his body as he waited for her answer. "I love you, Nick," she said softly, but despite her smile there was sadness in her golden eyes as she looked up at him. I cannot help myself, she thought; no matter how much he may hurt me, I will love him until I die.

Nick responded to her words with another kiss, swift and joyful, and then pulled her down to sit beside him on the bench. He kept one arm around her shoulder, as if he could not bear to break the contact between them.

"You make me so happy, darling, and I vow that I'll make you happy as well." Nick's voice mirrored his delight, and Amanda sighed as he caressed her ear with his long fingers. "It wouldn't do to take you to my house in London just now, but perhaps within a few weeks I can take you there, and deck you out in all the silks and jewels you deserve. I swear my friends will never believe I've snared myself such an Incomparable! I've got a house in St. James Square which is rather small, perhaps, but it is very well situated, and, of course, you can redecorate it any way you like."

Amanda had stiffened involuntarily at his words, feeling another stab of pain; the thought of London was almost more than she could bear. To be a mistress was one thing, but to be paraded openly, where there were distant relatives and acquaintances of the Waverley family! She mustered the courage to speak.

"I thought perhaps that we might live permanently abroad," she said hesitantly.

"What on earth for?" Nick looked down at her

with surprise. "We ought to return to the Continent for a few weeks longer, until that dueling affair dies down, but after that I'll want to return to England and home. Don't you feel the same?"

"Yes, but . . ." Her voice failed.

"But what?" Nick reached to take her chin in his hand, raising her eyes to meet his. He was startled to see them again clouded with tears. "What's the matter, my love?"

Her chin trembled in his hold. "I will do anything you wish, Nick; it's just that London is so—so public—"

He gazed at her searchingly for a moment; then when he spoke, his voice was very serious. "Amanda, I don't think you understand what it is that I wish. I don't want you only as my mistress. I want you as my wife."

She buried her face in his shoulder, her slender body shaking with emotion. It seemed too much like a dream, but as he gently stroked her hair, murmuring words of reassurance and love, the ache in her heart slowly ebbed away, and she dared to believe that this could all be true.

Nick let her weep softly for a few minutes, and then he gently pushed her away. "Of course, there's no saying I won't change my mind if you ruin my coat!" he teased gently.

She gave a watery laugh, dashing the tears out of her eyes, and then when he handed her a handkerchief, she blew her nose prosaically. His eyes glimmered with tender amusement as he looked down at her. "And besides," he added, "if you plan to become a watering-pot, you'd better say yes quickly before I decide to cry off."

"If I do marry you, Nick, does that mean you shall reform your wicked ways?" Her voice was half-mocking, half-serious.

He smiled at her in a way which made her heart turn over. "I promise never again to be wicked—except when you want me to be." And as he kissed her again, Amanda concluded with a shiver of delight that a little wickedness could be a very good thing indeed.